WARRIOR ANGEL

Also by Robert Lipsyte

THE CONTENDER

THE BRAVE

THE CHIEF

ONE FAT SUMMER

WARRIOR ANGEL

Robert Lipsyte

HarperCollins*Publishers*

Library of Congress
Cataloging-in-Publication Data
Lipsyte, Robert.
    Warrior angel / Robert Lipsyte.
        p.   cm.
    Summary: Native American boxer of the Moscondaga
Nation, Sonny Bear must fight to retain his heavyweight
championship title.
    ISBN 0-06-000496-7 — ISBN 0-06-000497-5 (lib. bdg.)
    [1. Boxing—Fiction.] I. Title.
PZ7.L67 War 2003   2002004551
[Fic]—dc21   CIP
                                                   AC

Typography by Henrietta Stern
1 2 3 4 5 6 7 8 9 10
❖
First Edition

FOR LOIS

One

INUTES BEFORE THE fight, Sonny Bear felt hollow. He lay on the padded table in the dressing room staring up at shapes moving across the ceiling like black storm clouds. He imagined his body the only tepee on a frozen meadow. His skin was stretched over the tent poles, pulled taut by wooden stakes in the hard earth. The tepee was empty. Nobody home.

He knew where such images came from, and he hated that place. Shove that tired old Redskin crap, I'm not anything anymore. Not Indian, not white. Leave me alone. I'm not anywhere.

The noise boiling around him seemed distant, as if it were coming from radios in passing cars. He tilted his head, peered from the corner of one eye.

His managers, Malik and Boyd, were sniffing like dogs around a short, heavily muscled man with a familiar face. It took Sonny a moment to recognize the actor who had killed a hundred alien invaders in the movie they had watched last night in the hotel room. Sonny had fallen asleep before the movie ended.

Across the room, facing a wall, Red Eagle chanted as he poured powders from leather sacks into a steel bowl. He struck a wooden match against the zipper of his jeans. Smoke rose from the bowl, and so did the stink of cow dung.

Sonny's trainer, checking the boxing gloves, cursed the smell. Two cornermen whose names Sonny couldn't remember rolled their eyes as they filled a metal pail with taped water bottles, jars of ointments, and cotton swabs. Sonny had given up trying to remember their names. They'd all be gone soon. Nobody lasts.

The movie star said, "Make it an early night, Sonny. I bet you in the third round." He cocked his forefingers and blasted aliens. He growled his big line from the movie: "Sayonara, snot-face." Malik and Boyd brayed like mules.

Sonny tried to wave at the movie star, but nothing moved.

The door banged open. A boxing commissioner marched in with a man wearing a REGGAE KING sweatshirt.

Sonny heard ringing bells, people yelling. The preliminary fights had started. He would have to go out soon. He wanted to sleep.

The commissioner said, "Hands, champ."

It took great effort to sit up and stretch out his hands.

"You okay, champ?" asked the commissioner.

It took Sonny a moment to realize the woman was talking to him. He nodded. I'm okay. Just not here tonight.

The man in the REGGAE KING sweatshirt said, "Let's see your hands." He checked the white tape around Sonny's knuckles, nodded, and watched Sonny's trainer, what-was-his-name, push the gloves on. After the laces were tied and taped over, the commissioner initialed the gloves and walked out. How many times have we done this? Sonny thought. But it seemed as though it were happening to someone else.

A famous rapper in a mink blazer came in, touched Sonny's glove, and introduced him to a woman whose black dress barely hung from her breasts.

"Ten minutes." An official glanced around the dressing room until someone nodded back at him, then slammed the metal door.

The rapper sang, "Ten more minutes you

3

will, uh-huh, make yourself another five mill, uh-huh." Malik and Boyd brayed and stroked his mink blazer.

The rapper, the woman in the black dress, and the short movie star left. The room quieted. Boyd began whispering into his cell phone. Malik sat on a stool and opened a skinny little laptop on his knees. "Sonny, up. E-mail from Nike wishing you luck. Reply?"

There were no words inside Sonny, no thoughts except the realization that he had no thoughts. He had always felt something before a fight. Until now.

"Stick it to Nike," said Boyd. "Remind 'em that sales on the Sonny Bear headbands are flat. Tell 'em we're talking direct to the Chinese."

Malik and Boyd touched thumbs and brayed in each other's face. Who are these fools, why are they here, why am I here?

Red Eagle had his long nose in the stinky smoke. What is he praying for now? A Nike deal to endorse powwow feathers?

A cameraman crouched in the middle of the room. He turned slowly, panning: Sonny sitting on the table, the fussing cornermen in their Sonny Bear T-shirts, Malik and Boyd in their red silk jackets, Red Eagle chanting as his hands caressed the rising smoke.

"Do not photograph this," said Red Eagle. He covered the camera lens with his hand. "It is sacred."

"It's part of the cable deal," said Boyd.

"It's okay," said the cameraman. "I got what I need."

What I need, thought Sonny, is a reason to go out there and beat some tomato can into a puddle of flesh.

"Sonny, up. You know a Warrior Angel?"

He shook his head, a cement block on his shoulders.

"He says he's coming," said Malik.

Red Eagle said, "Warrior Angel. What does he want?"

"He says he's coming to save Sonny."

"Check him out," said Boyd.

"Can't," said Malik. "It's a blocked address."

"What's it say?" asked Sonny.

"It says, *Dear George Harrison Bayer . . .*'"

"How's he know Sonny's real name?" asked Boyd.

"It's in that book—no big deal," said Malik. "Listen up. *Dear George Harrison Bayer. Do not lose heart. I come on a Mission from the Creator to save you.* It's signed, *Warrior Angel.*"

"The Creator speaks through me," said Red Eagle. He sounded angry.

"Exclusive deal, huh?" asked Malik.

"Is that funny to you?" snapped Red Eagle.

"Relax," said Boyd. "Sounds like a promotional stunt to get a title fight. Ask Warrior Angel if he's white. We need a white challenger, an American." He aimed a finger at the camerman. "Don't tape this."

Red Eagle looked serious. "Did that e-mail come to the web site or a private mailbox?"

"To champsonnybear."

Red Eagle relaxed. "It's nobody. Forget it."

Forget it, thought Sonny. Forget everything.

Two

STARKEY WAS ALMOST sorry he had bagged his meds this morning, clamping them between his cheek and gum while he chugged the orange juice. He had learned that trick in the hospital. The key was not to spit out the pills too soon. They watch for that. The longer you can keep them in your mouth, the better chance you have of getting away with it. He was having second thoughts about not taking the drugs. He had wanted to stay sharp for Sonny's fight, but now the faces in Circle were beginning to pulsate, and their voices were getting weird. He didn't want to chuck a ruckus and risk missing the fight. It would be starting in a few minutes. He had to get upstairs.

But he was losing it.

"Has everyone said hello to Starkey, welcomed our new family member?" Dr. Raphael smiled and nodded at him. The shrink was the only one in Circle sitting on a chair. A power thing, thought Starkey. The living-room floor was hard. He felt his underwear twist into his crack.

There were seven of them, mostly around his own age. The girls smiled a welcome, the boys nodded suspiciously.

"We're happy you're here," said Dr. Raphael. "Would you like to tell us a little about yourself?"

It was what the Archangels call a defining moment, a moment early in a Mission in which you can give it direction and establish your character.

I know enough to know I have choices. I can ask the doctor to cut me slack for now because I'm new here. Or I can make some wisecrack to get me off the hook.

Or I can go for it.

Go for it, he thought. Just remember that Warrior Angels never lie.

"I am a Warrior Angel, on a Mission for the Creator."

"Where are your wings?" That was Roger, big guy, fat but strong looking.

"Be a little obvious down here, don't you think?" said Starkey.

"What kind of Mission?" That was PJ, pretty girl, thin, wearing pajamas.

"This is an action job, my specialty," he said. He liked the look in her eyes. He started talking too much. "I was never one of your touchy-feely angels, all hope and inspiration, the Guardian Angels or, as we call them behind their backs, the Happy Haloes."

"Sounds like you got to put down other people to feel good about yourself." Tracey was a big girl, scars on her arm.

"C'mon, Tracey," said Roger, "are you buying into this psycho's fantasy?"

"Roger," said Dr. Raphael, "we make no judgments in Circle. Let's all hold hands and take a deep breath."

Starkey held his hands out. Dr. Raphael took Starkey's left hand in his dry, bony claw. PJ took his right. Her hand was soft and damp, and she rubbed her palm against his, sending a cascade of warmth down his chest, into his groin and legs. It felt good but it reminded him to stay focused. This group home is a perfect hideout, he thought, but these people aren't going to make it easy. Mental illness is a great disguise for a Warrior Angel; you can tell the truth and still be undercover. But you are dealing with unpredictable minds, genuine nutcases. Be glad to move on out of here into the Mission.

"Starkey, let's not talk for a moment," said Dr. Raphael.

He hadn't realized he'd been talking out loud. I have to remember how the Voices take over, he thought.

"Sure, blame it on voices," said Tracey.

Starkey concentrated on shutting down. He looked around the Circle. Most of the others had their eyes closed. PJ was smiling at him and Roger was glaring at both of them. So he was hot for her, and jealous. Live Ones are a problem. Have been, since the beginning of time.

"Well, would anyone like to talk about their day?" asked Dr. Raphael.

"I really hate going to school in the wacko wagon," said Tracey.

"That's because you think you're better than those other droolers and melonheads," said Roger. "But you're special ed and you better get used to it."

Tracey started to cry. The sound became a high-pitched whine that drilled into the back of Starkey's head.

"That was cruel," said PJ.

"That was truth," said Roger, "a commodity in short supply at the Family Place. You people can't handle the truth."

The rest of the Circle liked that. They banged their heels on the carpet, the only way to applaud when you are holding hands, thought Starkey. They probably hold hands a lot so they won't scratch their butts or pick their noses or try to feel each other up.

"Who you want to feel up?" asked Roger.

Dr. Raphael quickly said, "So what is this truth we can't handle, Roger?"

"That we're genuine nutcases, just like this genuine psycho said." He fired a forefinger at Starkey. "Down here on a Mission from God, huh? What for? Find yourself another movie star to stalk?"

"Wow." Tracy looked interested. "Who was it? How close you get?"

"Close enough to get busted, right?" said Roger.

"It was a mistake," said Starkey. That was true. Sonny was supposed to be at the party where he ran into the movie star. Security actually thought he was stalking some dumbo action hero.

Starkey tried to stay in the now, but he had

11

to keep track of the time. He checked his watch every minute. The fight would start soon. He didn't want to miss a second of it. He hoped Sonny had gotten his message, that it would give him strength. Sonny wasn't looking good. He was pale, dead eyed. He looked hollow, a shell of Sonny. On ESPN his voice had sounded even more of a monotone than usual. There were rumors on the internet he had the flu or something really bad.

"Don't listen to Roger," said PJ. "He gets off trying to bully people."

"Listen to America's victim," said Roger. "She and her sneaky little—"

"We're all glad you're here, Starkey, " said Dr. Raphael. "Aren't we?"

"Especially you, Doc," said Roger. "Another paying customer for the Family Circle jerk."

There was back and forth on that one, but Starkey smiled and nodded without paying attention. Don't need to get into their issues. Probably nice-enough people, he thought, troubled, sure, but decent, except for Roger, people trying to find their ways through their personal fogs. But I've got my own problem right now, got to get upstairs to see that fight.

He didn't realize he had spoken out loud again until Dr. Raphael said, "We don't feel good about boxing in the Family Place."

"Too violent," said PJ, shaking her head. Some of the others nodded. Roger smirked.

"Heavyweight championship of the world," said Starkey. "Everybody's going to be talking about it at school, and what am I going to say, 'Couldn't tune in because the shrink at the psycho retard nuthouse where I live thinks it might make me crazier'?"

Laughter, heel banging. Who says Warrior Angels don't have smooth moves? Even Roger winked at him.

Dr. Raphael smiled and said, "Could Starkey have a point?"

"If he did, he'd point it at PJ," said Roger.

Starkey took advantage of the sudden, embarrassed silence, dropped hands, and stood up. "Thank you very much. I understand this is a one-time privilege and I don't intend to abuse it."

He hurried upstairs before anyone could say anything more.

He just made it. The fight was about to start.

13

Three

A thought began to tug at the corner of Sonny's mind, but before he could decide whether or not to let it in, the door banged open and a voice boomed, "The world is waiting for Sonny Bear. Is Sonny Bear ready to deee-light the world with another deee-fense?"

Malik and Boyd jumped up and the trainer and the cornermen straightened. Even Red Eagle turned.

"Mind if I keep shooting, Mr. Hubbard?" asked the cameraman.

"My life is an open screen, dedicated to the cham-peen." Elston Hubbard gently slapped Sonny's cheeks. "Awake, my man, and prepare to pummel another pretender to the throne." He snapped his fingers at the trainer. "You know better. He should be warmed up by now."

"He won't do nothing, Mr. Hubbard," the trainer said.

Sonny watched as the big round dark face

loomed over him. He smelled Scotch and cigars. For once it didn't sicken him. Nothing. I am beyond feeling.

"Ten thousand people outside that door, Sonny, the cream of Las Vegas and Hollywood, and countless millions at home, waiting to be inspired anew by the Tomahawk Kid, the Natural Man, the Native Son. Can't disappoint." He grabbed Sonny's shoulders and pulled him off the table. He held up his hand. "Jab."

Sonny threw out a left. It felt as though he were punching through water.

"I said jab."

The second one was straighter but barely moved Hubbard's open hand. "Navy Crockett gonna think you are trying to pick his nose. JAB!"

He aimed this one at Hubbard's face and tried to remind his muscles to snap it out, to fire from the shoulder, to roll his wrist on impact.

Hubbard inclined his head, and the jab shot over his shoulder. "Better."

The cornermen took over, rubbing his arms, setting up targets. Sonny began jogging in place. He felt his muscles warming up, but they seemed detached from his brain. Someone else's muscles.

15

The door banged open. "Let's go. Crockett's in the ring."

"Showtime," said Hubbard. "Lead the way, Red Iggle."

It wasn't until they were out of the dressing room that Sonny realized they had been inside the health club of a casino hotel and were now crossing the pool area toward the parking lot. The air was warm, moist. He needed to breathe through his mouth as well as his nose.

Red Eagle, in the lead, scattered ashes from his steel bowl along a red carpet that ran through the crowd to the ring. They passed between two rows of young women in bikinis waving rubber tomahawks and shouting, "Son-nee, Son-nee."

Hubbard waved to the crowd, urged them to pick up the chant. Hands reached out to touch Sonny. He saw faces of people he knew, movie actors, rappers, ballplayers. Why were they here?

Navy Crockett was waiting in the ring, taller than Sonny and thirty pounds heavier, some of it fat. His upper arms jiggled when he shook them over his head. He spotted Sonny coming up the ring steps and glared.

As he climbed through the ropes, Sonny thought, What's his problem?

Sonny's robe was stripped off. The trainer ran an ice cube down his spine. He felt Hubbard's strong hands on his arm. "Snap out of it, Sonny. This . . . is for . . . your title."

Hubbard smacked him across the face, hard.

Sonny tried to will himself out of the brown murkiness that surrounded him, banging his gloves together, whipping his head from side to side so his ponytail slapped his bare shoulders. But the lines to his feelings had been disconnected.

The voice of the ring announcer could have come from another planet as he introduced the celebrities. They paraded across the ring, touched Crockett's gloves, touched Sonny's, wished both men luck. The former champion, Floyd (The Wall) Hall, raised his hands to the crowd. Lights glinted off a gold ring on every finger. The rapper glided across the ring to hug him. When the movie star trotted across the ring, the crowd shouted his alien-killer line from the movie: "Sayonara, snotface."

"And now, the main event, for the heavyweight championship of the world . . ."

The trainer's fingers were deep in the muscles of his shoulders, and the cornermen were kneading his legs.

"In the green trunks, the challenger, from Ja-mai-ca, at two hundred forty-one pounds, the Reggae King, Nay-veeeeee Crock-ett."

Steel drums pounded in the darkness at the back of the parking lot and a line of dancers snaked around the ring.

"In the red trunks, the pride of the Moscondaga Nation and of all Americans from Native to new, the youngest heavyweight champion in history, at two hundred ten pounds, the Tomahawk Kid, Son-neeeeeeeeeeee Bear."

War drums thundered, and the Tomahawk Girls shimmied down the aisle. Steel drums, war drums, the shouting dancers, the stars and the ballplayers and the rappers standing and cheering.

Sonny thought, I can't breathe.

Four

STARKEY THOUGHT SONNY LOOKED AWFUL, drugged, a robot.

He lurched out to the center of the ring, hands down, chin out. If Crockett hadn't been stiff with fear, he could have marched up and nailed him, ended the fight right then.

Look at those idiot managers, jumping up and down, yelling at Sonny to lift his hands, go after Crockett, chop that lard ass down. Do they want him to lose, or are they as stupid as the boxing writers say? They aren't much older than Sonny, punks who worked for that slimeball Hubbard. Why did Sonny let them in? Because he's losing his grip. Because he doesn't know who his real friends are. Because he needs me.

The crowd screamed for action.

PJ slipped onto the couch next to Starkey. "That was so cool, the way you got out of Circle. Which is the one you're rooting for?"

"Red trunks," said Starkey.

Roger plopped down. "Crockett's scared. Why doesn't Bear just put him away?"

Because I want all this to end, thought Starkey, thinking for Sonny, because I want to be free, to go back to sleep, to be alone.

A voice on the TV cut through the murk. "Navy, stick, stick and move, Navy."

"That guy used to train Sonny," said Starkey, "back when Alfred, Henry, and Jake were still in his corner." They didn't need to know all this. But he couldn't stop talking about Sonny. "That was all before Hubbard's punks took over."

"You know so much about him," said PJ.

"Starkey is obsessed with Sonny Bear," said Roger.

"We're not allowed to diagnose in the Family Place," said PJ.

"It's an observation, not a diagnosis," said Roger. "There are people who fixate on stars because of a lack in their own—"

"*Shut up!*" The words came out like straight rights and shut Roger right up.

A jab bounced off Sonny's forehead, just enough to shake him, not enough to hurt. Starkey felt pressure over his left eye.

Sonny looked blank, unfocused. Starkey imagined that Sonny's mind was wandering, seeing faces from his past floating in the crowd, attaching themselves to bodies, then moving on, like masks on strings. Mom and Doll and Robin, Alfred and Marty and Jake.

He imagined that Sonny felt dreamy now, surprised that his body could move on its own, as if it were acting out highlights from old fights. Remember how we kept moving to the left on Boatwright so he couldn't pull the trigger on his jab, in and out on Velez, who was dangerous but dumb.

One of the TV commentators said, "Crockett's got too much reach. Sonny has to move inside if he wants to win this."

"He's having trouble just keeping his hands up," said the other one.

"Sonny, look out," screamed the idiots in the corner.

Suddenly, Sonny was on the ring floor and the referee was pushing Crockett into a neutral corner. Starkey tried to feel Sonny's shock and pain, but felt only numbness. Was that all Sonny was feeling too?

The steel drums smothered the sound of

the referee's count, but Starkey could see him mouthing the numbers. "Two . . . three . . . four . . ."

"Up, Sonny, get up," screamed Starkey.

"Stay down, Sonny," said Roger. "You get up, it's just more of the same."

He wanted to slug Roger, as big as he was. He started to rise, felt PJ's body stiffen. He held the tension for a beat and thought, If Roger is a member of the Legion of Evil, if he is the adversary sent up from Hell to test me on this Mission, does it make sense to engage him now? Do you beat the devil early or late?

The bell rang.

"Sonny is saved by the bell," snorted Roger.

You, too, thought Starkey. I will not engage you now. This is about Sonny right now, not about me.

Hands dragged Sonny to his stool, snapped an ampule under his nose, poured ice water on his head, dropped a cube down the front of his trunks, massaged his arms and legs.

The camera moved in. Starkey saw the boom mike, a fuzzy fat gray caterpillar hovering over Sonny's head, picking up the conversation in his corner.

"Wake up, Sonny." The trainer was slapping his face.

"What's your name?" A man in a suit and tie. The ring doctor.

"Sonny Bear."

"Where are you?"

"Las Vegas."

"Who you fighting?"

"Navy Crockett."

The doctor shrugged and walked away.

One of the idiot managers said, "Sonny, you got to back off—"

But the other idiot said, "In his face, get right up in Crockett's face—"

And then the trainer said, "Tie him up."

Too many voices in Sonny's ear, Starkey thought, when all he needs is mine. He said, "Just hang on."

"For dear life." Roger laughed.

The bell rang.

Bolder now, Crockett marched right up and fired a jab. Some distant memory must have jogged Sonny to slip the punch, let it fly harmlessly over his shoulder, to ram a short right uppercut into Crockett's soft belly.

"Huuunh." Crockett doubled over, his chin

slamming into Sonny's shoulder. Sonny grabbed him, pulled him into a clinch. Crockett wrenched loose and stumbled away.

The fear was back. Crockett circled again. The movie stars and rappers and ballplayers stamped their cowboy boots and chanted, "Son-nee, Son-nee."

Behind them, to the steel-drum beat, voices from the cheaper seats chanted, "Nay-vee, Nay-vee."

Starkey could sense that Sonny's murkiness never completely cleared and that he never quite connected with his body, even when he got his hands up and began to move his feet. Twice he caught Crockett coming in with sharp jabs. The second time he managed to land a hook as Crockett was backing away. It startled Crockett, and he tripped over his feet, falling on his backside. He was up again before the referee could start the count, but he stayed away from Sonny for the rest of the round.

The crowd began to boo through the middle rounds as the fight fell into a pattern. Crockett would circle until he gathered enough courage to attack. He might land a jab or two, even a brief flurry of punches, but Sonny would trap his arms and step into a clinch.

The referee broke them apart as quickly as he could, "No hugging—fight," but Crockett couldn't stop Sonny from clinching.

One of the TV commentators said, "Navy's too slow, too set in his ways to figure this out."

"He's a classic plodder willing to absorb punches to give some back," said the other. "But Sonny's hardly mounting any offense at all. Wasn't this supposed to be a just a little tune-up fight for the champ?"

At the beginning of the tenth, Starkey sensed Sonny's murk beginning to lift, like a stage curtain slowly rising. He could see that Sonny felt it first in his arms, lighter, then in his feet, moving faster. Sonny snapped three straight jabs into Crockett's face, driving him back across the ring, and as the crowd began to roar, he slammed a left hook into Crockett's jaw and a vicious short right into his heart. Crockett fell against the ropes, his elbows snagged on the top strand. The crowd was on its feet as Sonny lowered his head and pounded Crockett's soft gut.

"Kill the body and the head will die," shouted Starkey.

Roger snickered. "Where you hear that dopey stuff?"

Starkey started to rise, but PJ squeezed his arm and he settled back down. It was in The Book. Mr. Donatelli had spoken those words to Alfred, who had passed them on to Sonny. Can't react to Roger, not now.

Crockett had nothing left, he was in no condition to box for twelve rounds, and he sucked air and circled until the final bell sounded. The crowd was booing and whistling. It got louder after the ring announcer pulled down the mike and read the judges' cards.

Split decision. Sonny wins, retaining the title.

Starkey felt sweet warm relief fill his chest.

"Crockett got robbed," said Roger. "And your guy is almost as screwed up as you are."

"Get lost," snapped Starkey.

Roger stood up. "Make me, psycho pup."

Defining moment, now or never. Starkey stood up. He tried to imagine what Sonny would do, but before he could even think it through, the heel of his hand shot out and slammed into Roger's nose. Roger sat down hard, blood leaking between his fingers.

Roger whimpered. "I'm gonna tell—"

"And I'll say you bothered me," said PJ. "Now get lost, toad."

PJ didn't wait for Roger to leave before she sat down and hugged Starkey. He was too surprised to resist. Besides, he knew Roger would snitch to Dr. Raphael that he had hit him and they'd send a counselor up.

Then I can get back to my room and send Sonny another message. He closed his eyes and wrote it in his mind: *Dear George Harrison Bayer, Saw you on TV after the fight. That look in your eyes, like it's hopeless. It's not. Hang on. I'll be there as soon as I can. Warrior Angel.*

Five

THE BOOING ROLLED over the ring. He met Crockett in the middle and they hugged.

"I stunk," said Sonny, patting Crockett's back. "Sorry."

"Me, too, mon."

He shuffled back to his dressing room.

Hubbard was bellowing at the trainer, "Pack your sack, never want to see your face again."

Malik jerked a thumb at the cornermen. "And take those useless—"

Hubbard growled, "Malik, shut your mouth. 'Cept to thank me for letting you pretend to be the manager."

Malik and Boyd slunk across the room.

Red Eagle said, "There is a dark spirit inside the young brave. . . ."

Hubbard whirled on him. "So get your mojo on it. That's why I give you the big wampum."

Sonny climbed up on the table and stretched out.

Hubbard's face bobbed over him. "No media. I can keep the vultures out."

"Don't care."

Hubbard's face came close. "That wasn't you out there, Sonny." He turned and raised his voice. "Sonny was drugged. Only explanation. Never been so sluggish before. You all got that?"

Malik and Boyd looked at each other, and Boyd blurted, "We didn't—"

"That's right you didn't—do nothing. Okay, let 'em in."

Hubbard stood in front of the table, arms crossed, blocking Sonny as the camera crews led the charge into the dressing room. Hubbard ignored their shouted questions until the pack had settled down, cameras rolling, pens poised above notebooks.

"Tomorrow morning," he said, "I will demand the boxing commission investigate drugs infiltrated into the champion's food or water."

"Are you accusing—"

"The commission will accuse, the Good Lord may excuse, all I say. That wasn't the Sonny Bear we know out there."

A TV reporter said, "He was sleepwalking out there."

"Pre-cisely," said Hubbard. "And he could have got killed. We have a case gonna rock boxing. Count on you people to keep the commission's feet to the fire, don't let them sweep it under the floor."

"Sonny, what do you think?"

Hubbard stepped aside. The bobbing faces made Sonny dizzy. "Felt flat. Couldn't get off."

"You think you were drugged?"

He sat up. "Don't know what it was."

"Try this," said one of the TV reporters into his camera. "Is Sonny Bear over the hill at twenty?"

There was a moment of silence, then Hubbard boomed, "We will find out in six weeks. I have an announcement."

The reporters pressed forward again.

"A year ago Sonny Bear snatched the title in one of the greatest wars of modern times. He will now defend his title against that fearsome warrior."

"The Wall?" someone asked.

"Who can forget? Floyd (The Wall) Hall is coming out of retirement to attempt to reclaim his throne." Hubbard pointed to the dressing-room door. "The Wall is across the hall, waiting to talk to you."

The pack turned and rushed away.

A reporter with a familiar face lingered. "Not much time, six weeks."

Hubbard nodded. "Strike while the public still hot."

"You mean before your deal with Sonny runs out."

Sonny slipped past them into the shower room. He lost track of time under the hot needle spray.

"Sonny." It was the trainer. He was holding towels. "You okay? Better drink lotsa water."

"Thanks." He stepped out and let the trainer wrap the towels around him.

"That's it for me, Sonny. Hubbard canned me."

"Sorry. Good luck."

"I'll be okay. Good luck to you, kid. Take care of yourself." The man didn't seem to want to leave. "Get yourself some help."

"Help?"

"Talk to somebody, know what I mean?"

"You still here?" Red Eagle stood at the

shower-room door.

The trainer hurried away.

Sonny dried off and dressed slowly. Get help, the trainer said. What did he mean? Who could he talk to? Red Eagle, Malik, and Boyd were still in the dressing room. Talk to those three stooges? Malik was staring into the laptop screen.

"That guy is back, the Warrior Angel."

"What's he say now?" asked Sonny. He was surprised at his interest.

"Crazy stuff," said Malik.

"Read it," said Sonny.

"*Dear George Harrison Bayer, Saw you on TV after the fight. That look in your eyes, like it's hopeless. It's not. Hang on. I'll be there as soon as I can. Warrior Angel.*"

I am deep in the murk, Sonny thought, and the Warrior Angel is on his way.

By the time they got to the victory party, on the top floor of the Oasis Hotel, the guests had cleaned off the buffet tables. Malik and Boyd grumbled, but Sonny wasn't hungry. Red Eagle squatted on his heels in a corner, eating dried fruits and grains from the pouches that hung from his shoulders. The short, muscled movie star came over to taste Red Eagle's food and drew a crowd.

Sonny drifted around the big room. He moved whenever he saw someone coming to talk to him. The waiters, their heads shrouded in the hotel staff's Arabian Nights costumes, appeared as ghostly as he felt.

At a wall of windows, he looked down at the Vegas Strip. He remembered the first time he had ever seen it, flying in from New York with Marty Witherspoon. He had thought then the Strip looked like all the crayons in the world melted into a dazzling river. Marty had liked that image, and Marty was a writer.

Beyond the colors was the darkness of the desert. He had a sudden urge to get out, to run the wind.

He heard raised voices behind him.

"You have really got some stones coming in here." The movie star, legs spread, hands on hips, was glaring up at the rapper.

"Little man, you don't know stones, uh-huh, so watch you mouth or I snap your bones, uh-huh." The rapper laughed and high-fived his bodyguards.

A circle formed around the rapper and the movie star. The party quieted down. Casino security officers began whispering into their headset mikes. Sonny waited until he spotted Malik and Boyd crowding in before he began backing out toward the nearest service elevator. The waiters were leaving their posts to watch.

"You must feel lucky, loudmouth," snarled the movie star. His hands were high, the position he used to bust up aliens.

"Short story, you would make me shake, uh-huh, if a real fight was more than one take, uh-huh."

When the movie star went into his kick-boxing spin, Sonny bolted for the elevator. The service area was deserted. He was in the elevator, door closing, as the crowd began roaring. Sounds like a better fight than mine, he thought.

No one paid him attention in the basement kitchen, and then he was out in the night, jogging along the Strip, weaving around clumps of tourists and couples holding hands and families with babies in strollers. The crowd thinned, disappeared. The neon river was behind him. He ran through clusters of suburban homes, and then he was on a two-lane blacktop, the only light from moon and stars.

Sonny ran.

The headlights of approaching cars and

trucks blinded him. Sprayed pebbles hit him like buckshot. Even so, the darkness of the desert comforted him, the cool of the night was a blanket. Animals scurried over the sandy rocks. Friends running with him.

He loved to run. It was the best part of training. Especially running alone. Early in the morning or late at night, body still stiff from sleep or sore from a tense day, he would start slow, anticipating the warmth rising from his feet, drowning the aches, finally reaching his brain and flushing the thoughts away.

He pulled the bands off his ponytail, felt his hair fall loose on his shoulders, then lift as the air flowed past his face. He imagined the strands of his hair spread out behind him, the flaps of the tent free from the stakes.

He was no longer alone. He heard a familiar whirring noise. A wheelchair pulled up alongside him.

"You blew it, Sonny," said Alfred. "You had it all, and you blew it."

"I had to be free," said Sonny.

"From people who cared about you?"

"Nobody really cares about me, just use me 'cause I'm the champ."

On the other side of him, Marty said, "Now

you're free? To do what Hubbard wants? To hang around with those two jerks and that phony Indian?"

"I should hang around with you? So you can write another book?"

Sonny ran away from them.

What did they know, a crippled black cop who never made it as a boxer and a fat black college boy who wrote about life instead of living it? What did they know about what was inside him, the monster he had to tame and the dark shadow he couldn't always push away? They always thought all I had to do was show up and train and listen to them and everything would be all right.

Once I thought so too.

It was easier to get to be champion than to stay champion, all these people pulling at you, telling you what to do, where to be, how to dress, now that you're a role model, a money machine, the king. King of what?

Nobody knows what I feel inside.

"I knew," said Jake. "When you were a Running Brave."

"I was never a Running Brave."

"In your heart." He couldn't believe the old

man was keeping up with him. Jake was dead. His heart had given out one day while he was working in his auto junkyard on the reservation. Just a few months ago. Seemed like years. "Not no more. Running Braves run to something. You just running away."

Sonny ran away from him.

He was alone again in the night. He had had it and he had blown it. So what, who cares? Just run. Keep running until you can't run anymore, then lie down in the desert and go to sleep. Forever. Nobody cares. Hubbard's got contracts with the Reggae King and The Wall. Promotors always make money. He'll take care of Malik and Boyd, and Red Eagle can go back to suckering rich people in his phony sweat lodges. Never miss me.

Nobody'll miss me.

Except Warrior Angel. Some nutcase fan out there, drunk, maybe whacked out on Warrior Angel Dust. That's funny. Warrior Angel Dust. Marty always told people, Sonny'll surprise you with a great line now and then. Sonny's smarter than you think. Marty was all right. But he's gone. Ran away from him, too.

The sky exploded, a dazzling beam of light

and a metallic clatter. He was staggered by a sandstorm. It took him a moment to realize that a helicopter was hovering overhead. Booming voices calling him to stop.

Ahead, flashing red lights. Police cars. Somebody *had* missed him. Too late. Doesn't matter anymore.

He jumped a drainage ditch and cut into the desert, stepping high to avoid rocks and weeds. The chopper followed, trapping him in its beam of light. He looked for hiding places in rock formations or groves of trees, but the land was tabletop flat here. He couldn't shake free of the light.

One of the police vehicles was bumping over the desert toward him now, its siren screaming through the clattering rotors.

The monster rose. Go for it, Sonny, you can beat 'em, outrun them all, go, Sonny, go, and then the dark shadow beat its wings and the murk returned and he stopped and fell to his knees.

Six

THEY CAME DOWN to get him in a green Land Rover, not Mom's red Beemer, not the stepmobile, which was what Starkey called his stepfather's big blue Benz. The Land Rover. Did they think they were setting out on a dangerous jungle journey, psychos leaping out of the bushes and landing on the hood?

PJ was watching from the front window. "Are they coming in?" She was wearing pajamas as usual. It was why they called her PJ. "I'd like to meet them."

"We're in kind of a hurry." Starkey wondered why she would want to meet them.

"We could be special friends, Starkey."

The Archangels go ballistic when Warrior Angels get involved with Live Ones without their permission. It happens, of course, but it's a conflict of interest. Worse than that, it almost always interferes with the Mission.

He tried to cut them off at the door so they

wouldn't snoop around the house, wouldn't see PJ.

"Richard!" Mom had her arms out. Starkey couldn't stop her from wrapping him up.

Stepdad was a step behind her. He was dressed all in black, as usual these days. Big phony smile revealed pointy teeth. His eyes changed from blue to purple to red back to blue. Starkey had bagged the morning meds again.

"You look terrific." Everything was always about looks with him. I could be rotting inside, Starkey thought, but if my hair is combed, everything's fine. "This place must agree with you. Ready to roll?"

"Sure." He hoisted his backpack and started for the door, but Mom spotted PJ.

"Hello."

"Hi. You must be Starkey's mother," said PJ. "I'm his friend Allysse."

Starkey got right in between them. "We're running late, Mom."

"Excuse my appearance," said PJ, "but I've gained a lot of weight lately and I haven't been able to shop."

Mom's face fell apart at that. PJ was slim, so it was clear to her that PJ had an eating problem. "Congratulations, sweetheart. I know how hard it is to gain weight when you have a . . . food issues."

"I wish my parents were as understanding as you," said PJ. "Starkey has told me all about you and your husband."

Starkey was surprised at her moves. He hadn't told her anything. What was she angling for?

"We're very proud of Richard." Stepdad moved closer to PJ. She didn't move away. What is her game? Starkey felt helpless. Their voices began to fade in and out, as if bubbling up from the bottom of a toilet.

"Weee're going to the mawllllllll," said Mom, "to get Richard a new shirt and tie. Come with ussssss. . . ."

"That's so nye-sssssssssssssss, but I cooon't innnnn-troooood. . . ."

"Yooooooo muuuuuust. . . ." Mom had PJ's arm and was steering her toward the office.

Nooooooo. They would get permission for PJ to come, ruin his plan.

Stepdad was pushing him out the door. "You all right, Richard? Look a little shaky."

"You don't have to hold me. I'm not crazy."

"I know that. You have a chemical imbalance that makes you do crazy things, Richard, and we're working on it."

"Work on this." He gave Stepdad the finger salute.

Stepdad ignored the gesture and guided him into the back of the Land Rover with his hand on top of his head, the way cops did it. Inside, the Land Rover smelled of leather, air-conditioning, perfume, after-shave.

"That's a foxy lady, Allysse. What's she in for?" Stepdad watched himself in the rearview mirror as he slipped on little round dark glasses.

"Biting off her father's nose."

That shut him up. Stepdad slipped in a CD, probably one of the new groups he was pushing. They just listened to the lame music until Mom reappeared, holding PJ's hand. Stepdad whistled. PJ did look good. Boots, tight black jeans, a black leather jacket, her hair pulled back. Lipstick and eyeliner. She climbed in next to Starkey and smiled at him.

"Nothing fits, huh?" said Starkey.

"Doesn't Allysse look wonderful," said Mom, settling into the front passenger seat.

"It's so nice of you to include me," said PJ.

"Your mother seemed very happy to give permission," said Mom. "She sounded lovely on the phone."

"Your dad?" Stepdad pulled slowly out of the parking lot, squinting at PJ in the rearview. Starkey thought his nose was twitching.

"My dad? He's on TV, travels a lot."

Stepdad glared at Starkey in the rearview. Starkey bit his lip so he wouldn't laugh out loud. He loved to pull the stepchain.

Mom turned in her seat. Her voice rose and fell in an oscillating wave, the highs like screeching brakes, the lows like the growls of animals trapped in a stinking circus cage. The sounds hammered him against the back of the seat.

"Yooooooo can help ussssssssss find a tiiiii-eeeee for Rich-chard."

"I'd love tooooooooooo."

Starkey tried to shake his head, but it felt locked in place. It was getting hard to breathe. He never thought Mom was Legion before, but now he wondered.

That helped. Wondering.

Centered him.

Caught his breath.

Stepdad said, "Yo! Locs 'n' Bagels' newest cut."

"He just loves this group." Mom rolled her eyes until only the whites showed, then they turned black. "He invented them." She rubbed Stepdad's thigh while he drove and hummed along.

Starkey hated to see that. So he thought instead about Sonny on the morning TV shows, hollow eyed when they brought him back from his midnight run. Dad might have looked like that before he crashed.

If Sonny had been driving instead of running . . .

They started talking again once the song was over, but he tuned it out. PJ started rubbing his thigh the same way Mom rubbed Stepdad's, but he blocked thinking about that by thinking about Sonny.

Sonny wouldn't give any interviews, but Elston Hubbard, that fat snake, gave dozens, spinning the same story over and over, how Sonny had been so shamed by his performance against Crockett that he needed to take a ritual cleansing run into the desert to purge the evil spirits in preparation for his next defense, against Floyd (The Wall) Hall. In all the TV interviews, the phony Indian, Red Ugly, was right behind him, nodding all the way. The sportscasters didn't have the guts to ask them why they had to send helicopters and police cars after Sonny. Or even to follow up on Hubbard's story that he had been drugged. Hubbard owned them, too.

Sonny was battling evil spirits all right, but you need more than a little run in the desert to defeat them. Hang in there, Sonny. I'm on my way.

He felt calmer by the time they got to the bottom of the long driveway, calm enough not to feel the windmill in his chest that usually started turning when the white stone mansion loomed into sight. The first time the town cops drove him home, whacked out of his mind behind the steel grate in the backseat of the cruiser, he'd yelled, "Welcome to the slammer." He had never again looked at the big house on the reservoir without thinking he was being returned to prison.

"What a lovely house," cried PJ.

*　　*　　*

The housekeeper opened the door and hugged him—"Reee-chid, I miss you"—and bustled him inside. Lunch was waiting at the pool, plates and silver and linen napkins in ivory rings. At the Family Place they ate like animals, with their hands. Food tastes better when you're not self-conscious, he thought. Maybe that's why so many rich girls are anorexic and bulimic, their parents are so hung up on table manners. It screws up the food and then it screws you up.

PJ hummed and oohed over everything but mostly pushed her food around the plate. Stepdad was on two cell phones through lunch. He kept apologizing, but he was in the process of forcing some record-store chain to put Locs 'n' Bagels posters in their windows or he'd cut them out of some other deal and maybe eat their children.

Starkey thought, Why am I here?

"What an awful question," said Mom.

"What?"

"Why are you here. We're your family, Richard. We love you and care about you."

Starkey began to laugh. "Sorry. I didn't realize I'd left the microphone on again."

Stepdad began yelling into both phones, showing off, and Starkey just nodded as Mom made small talk. She told PJ about Starkey's sisters, half sisters really, both away at boarding school. Amy made the lacrosse team, blah-blah, Kate has the lead in an original rap opera written by an African-American student that Jeremy's company was sponsoring. She didn't tell PJ that the black kids' scholarship was part of the deal to get their two halfwit daughters into the school. Then there was gossip about neighbors Starkey barely remembered. The husband had run off with the pool boy. PJ nodded as if she were interested.

He slipped away and went upstairs. His old room was just the way he had left it when the judge had sent him to the Whitmore Hills Juvenile Correctional Facility after that bogus arson bust. When the librarian had stopped him from taking out all three of copies of *The Tomahawk Kid,* he'd had to burn them so The Book wouldn't fall into the wrong hands. He was never trying to burn down the library.

He hadn't minded Whitmore too much. Wising off to Capt. Deeks had gotten him a week in solitary but gave him creds in the general population. The skinheads protected him from the blacks and the Latinos until one of them made Redskin jokes while they were watching a documentary on Sonny and he wouldn't shut up until Starkey put a ballpoint between his ribs. The next time Starkey came out of solitary, the skinheads ambushed him in the latrine and he was lucky to escape with only a slashed arm.

It worked out fine. Stepdad's lawyers used that to spring him out of Whitmore and into the hospital. Where they wanted to zap his brains. Electroconvulsive therapy was back in style. It was the only time Starkey felt scared. It would mean not only aborting the Mission but not returning to Heaven. Electroshock breaks communications between a Warrior Angel and the Archies. He would forget he was an angel. He would be stranded on Earth for a natural life, just another Live One.

Stepdad was all for it, zap the kid, but Mom wasn't sure. Maybe she'd seen the movie *One Flew Over the Cuckoo's Nest*. Maybe Dad had been zapped. They did it a lot in those days. The hospital came up with an alternative—one of its doctors ran a group home for adolescents, the Family Place. It was near where they lived in

Connecticut. Last chance before we microwave your boy.

And here we are, sports fans, back in the family place, lower case, please.

The Sonny Bear posters were beginning to curl at the edges—he would have to repin them. The Sonny Bear headbands were made-in-China junk, but you have to support your man.

"There you are." Mom came into the room. He could hear Stepdad booming at PJ downstairs. "We wondered where . . ."

He pulled the Sonny Bear fringed buckskin jacket out of the closet. "I'll wear this to the club tonight," he said.

His mother's face tightened; she caught her breath but then decided to smile. "I was hoping you'd let me buy you a new shirt and tie to go with your good blazer. This is really important to your father."

"My father's dead—he won't care."

She sighed, then decided not to go there. "Then for me, Richard, please."

"Can I drive?"

That stopped her. "Well . . ."

"The Land Rover."

She took a very deep breath. She hated the

49

buckskin jacket. If he wore it to the club tonight, their uptight friends would think he was still cuckoo. A blue blazer with brassy buttons, well, that's an obvious proof of sanity.

"All right, Richard. You can drive, once we're out of town. If the local police see you . . ."

"No problem."

He waited until he heard her footsteps going downstairs before he pried open the secret compartment in the back of his closet. Everything was still there: the cap, The Book, and the money belt. He tried the cap on, a red Tomahawk Kid baseball cap, very rare, before he slipped it into the backpack next to the laptop. He didn't like to wear it unless he really needed to block the Voices—you can't take a chance of using up its powers.

He strapped the money belt around his waist. It was stuffed with cash. Smartest thing he'd ever done. The getaway fund, he called it. Stepdad, showing off, was always leaving his money clip around. So long as you didn't take more than a fifty at a time, he would never notice. He used fifties as tips the way most people used fives.

His copy of *The Tomahawk Kid*, by Martin Malcolm Witherspoon, was falling apart, he had read it so many times, marked so many lines. He ran his fingers over the binding. You needed to know exactly where to feel to find the razor blade. He put The Book in an outer pocket by itself.

He shrugged into the backpack. I've got everything I need now to save Sonny.

Big shot was on both cells and a speaker-phone when they left. Still, he managed to wave to them, with an extra pinky wiggle for PJ. She wiggled her pinky back. Mom giggled like a girl. It made Starkey sick.

"Are you bringing your laptop to the mall?" asked Mom.

"I never go anywhere without it," he said. "It's my security blanket."

PJ climbed into the back of the Rover, cooing at the upholstery. What's her game? Her parents have a Jag and a Hummer.

He'd never been up front. The command perch was awesome. He wondered if there were psychological studies on what it does to your hormone level. Look down on everything, see what's going on in other cars, feel superior to everyone.

Out of town, just before the parkway, Mom pulled off the road. Without a word they both

got out and switched seats. It felt more like driving Stepdad's boat than a car. He forced himself
to concentrate on the road and to ignore the
faces in other cars. They would try to distract
him, make him wreck. Not this time.

The parking lot at the mall was crowded.
Mom said she wanted to start at the men's
store.

"I'll drop you two off there," said Starkey,
"park, and meet you inside."

"Well, I . . ." Mom seemed a little flustered.
He could tell she really didn't want him out of
her sight with the car.

"You don't trust me, do you? All the talk
about how much progress I'm making is just
talk. You don't think I'm not making any
progress at all, do you?"

"That's not true. You're doing so well . . .
but . . ." She turned in her seat. "I'm sorry,
Allysse, I don't mean for you—"

"Trust is something we talk about a lot in
Circle," said PJ.

That put her on the ropes. One big punch
and the match was his. "It's all front, isn't it,
Mom, blue blazer with brass buttons so you can
show me off at the club—see, Richard's not a

nutjob retard psycho loony, he's just fine, just like my perfect daughters. But you don't really think so, do you?"

She sighed; tears welled in her eyes. She's on the canvas, the ref's counting her out. Will she get up?

"I'll stay with Star . . . um, Richard, while he parks," said PJ.

That nailed it. PJ and Mom exchanged meaningful glances. "I'll be in the men's store— meet you by the ties." She kissed his cheek and quickly got out.

He felt a moment of sadness. She would never trust him again. But the Mission came first. Sonny needed him.

He waited until she had disappeared into the mall before he turned to PJ in the back. "Thanks, PJ, I owe you one. I can drop you off at—"

"I'm going with you, Starkey." She was already climbing into the front seat.

"I'm going to Las Vegas."

"Cool."

Seven

SONNY WAS PICKING at a room service hamburger and watching a baseball game with Malik and Boyd when Hubbard marched in with a stranger and announced, "Meet the top jock doc from the university, Dr. Gould."

Sonny looked up at a round-faced man with a bushy mustache. "What's this about?"

"Think we should talk to a pro-fessional," said Hubbard. "The new mot-to in sports: You gotta get shrunk to get bigger."

Sonny started to shake his head, tell them all to take a hike, when Malik said, "You think Sonny needs a psychiatrist?" and Boyd said, "That's crazy," and they laughed their stupid laugh.

Sonny stood up. Talk to the man just to get away from the fools.

The doctor motioned Sonny to follow him into the bedroom.

"The first time," said Hubbard, "should be a

family affair. We are all—"

"My patient is Sonny, not the family." He closed the bedroom door and dragged two upholstered chairs to face each other.

"No couch?" asked Sonny sarcastically.

"You can use the bed if you like." He sat down.

Sonny sat in the other chair. He looked the doctor in the eyes with the cold glare he used to psych opponents during the ring instructions and was surprised to find him looking right back, friendly, interested. Not intimidated.

"Have you been in therapy before?" asked the doctor.

"Physical therapy," said Sonny.

"There are similarities. We start with the premise that the pain you are feeling is a symptom of something that's wrong, at least out of balance. We work on it, sometimes causing more pain but moving toward the cause and hopefully . . ."

"I couldn't get started," said Sonny. "Couldn't get combinations going."

"What were you feeling?"

"Frustrated."

"At what?"

"I been through all this. Read it in the papers."

"Why'd you come in here with me if you don't want to talk to me?" It was an honest question, Sonny thought, no nasty edge to it.

Tell him the truth, see what he does with it. "Get away from them."

Doc was cool, didn't try to use that to make friends with Sonny. He just nodded. "Okay, you said you were frustrated. What were you thinking?"

"That I didn't know why I felt like that."

"Like what?"

He could hear Hubbard and his donkeys braying outside. Might as well talk to this man a little. "Everything was heavy, slowed down. I pulled a muscle once, and Henry Johnson had me punch underwater while it healed. It felt like that."

"Did you think of anything else then?"

"In the middle of a fight?"

"Other places, people, feelings you had? Pictures in your head?"

Sonny remembered the floating faces in the crowd, Mom and Doll and Robin, Alfred and Marty and Jake. This wasn't going to work. He

56

didn't want to talk about them.

"We don't need to talk about this right now," said Dr. Gould, as if he read Sonny's mind. "Take me through the fight, as much detail as you can remember."

That was easy. He did it by himself all the time anyway. The fight was stored like a videotape on a shelf in his brain with all his fights. He let it unwind slowly. Dr. Gould stopped him from time to time, trying to get him to remember a feeling, a flash of memory, but he had none he wanted to share. He plowed on, boring himself, punch by punch. It must have been a boring fight to watch, he thought.

When he finished, Dr. Gould leaned back in his chair, raked his mustache with his fingers, and said, "You know, if this were purely a mechanical problem, you could go back to the gym and work it out with your trainer."

"You think it's in my head?"

"You ever read about the major league catcher who had trouble returning the ball to the pitcher? There was also a case of a basketball player who suddenly started throwing bricks from the foul line. Athletes often act out their emotional problems athletically."

"So what's my problem?" He heard his voice from a distance, tossing out a challenge.

"I don't know. You haven't told me."

"You're the doctor."

The doctor stood up. "That's all we have time for today."

"Just like that?" He was sorry it was over.

Dr. Gould said, "When the bell rings, time's up."

Hubbard was waiting outside the door. Sonny wondered if he had tried to eavesdrop. "So, Doc, what's he say?"

"That's private, between Sonny and me."

"I'm paying you."

"Talk to Sonny." He walked around Hubbard and left.

Hubbard walked into the bedroom. "So?"

Sonny shrugged and climbed into bed with the remote. Hubbard stared at him and shook his head before he left. The baseball game was still on. Sonny watched the catcher throw the ball back to the pitcher. He remembered reading about the catcher who suddenly couldn't throw the ball back to the pitcher. Guy was a head case. Am I a head case? His stomach hurt. He pushed the thought away.

"Let us chant," said Red Eagle, slipping silently into the room. He might or might not be a real Indian, but he moved like one. He was sprinkling powders into the steel bowl.

"Not now. And get that dung out of here."

"You had time for the white man's healer. Do you think his medicine is stronger than the medicine of the Creator?"

Sonny grunted and rolled over on his stomach.

He dozed for a while. The TV in the living room woke him up. A western. He could hear Indian war whoops and gunfire. Only Boyd was stupid enough to watch that here. He walked out into the living room.

"Where's Malik's laptop?"

"In his room, I guess. But he don't like—"

"Right." He found it blinking on Malik's bed, two animated kick boxers, naked women, whaling each other on the screen saver. He took it back to his room.

It took him a while to make his way through the porn sites that Malik had programmed to pop up at first touch. There was a New Mail message at his public e-mail address, champ-sonnybear@aol.com, from the Warrior Angel.

Dear George Harrison Bayer,
Getting closer, but not moving as the
Hawk flies. Too dangerous. Hang on.
Warrior Angel

How did he know about the Hawk?

It was in the book *The Tomahawk Kid*, by Martin Malcolm Witherspoon, a book that told too much and nothing at all. Why had he let that fat black owl rip him off, write a book that exposed him but didn't set him free?

Where was Marty now?

He heard Boyd and Malik talking, then Malik's heavy steps toward the bedroom door. Sonny back-paged to one of the porn sites.

"Hey, man, whatchoo doon' wit' my . . ." Malik came around behind Sonny just as the screen filled with flesh. He grinned. "Feelin' better, huh?"

Food had no taste. Time stood still, a puddle of stagnant water. Hubbard had a treadmill brought up to the hotel room, and Sonny jogged on it for hours at a time, trying to imagine himself on a road in the Res. Then he'd sit in front of the TV for hours, watching the screen turn into a kaleidoscope of meaningless colors.

Dr. Gould came again. The sessions broke loose old memories. Moving from the Reservation near Sparta in Upstate New York to Boston to Minneapolis to Santa Fe to Santa Cruz, California, as a kid while his mother tried to sell the jewelry she designed and made. Always coming back broke to the Res and his great-uncle Jake's auto junkyard. Hiding in the backs of old wrecked cars, drawing pictures he tore up before anyone could see them. Helping Jake find parts in the old cars for his customers. Dropping out of Sparta High School after he was kicked off the football team. He had slugged a teammate, an elephant-assed tackle who had called him Tonto. Didn't like football anyway. Too many rules. A white man's game.

He didn't tell Gould any of it.

He remembered running away to Times Square, falling in with Doll and her pimp, Stick, getting busted by Sgt. Alfred Brooks. Once, he'd thought that was the best thing that had ever happened to him. Now, he wasn't so sure of anything.

He felt trapped in the hotel suite, a prisoner.

He felt as helpless as he had at the Whitmore Hills Juvenile Correctional Facility. That was almost three years ago.

He had a dream.

He was walking backward up to Donatelli's Gym, slowly, feeling each step sag under his weight, hearing the old wood creak. He knew that Mr. Donatelli himself was waiting at the top of the three dark, narrow flights of stairs, and he knew the old man would be disappointed because it wasn't Alfred. He was waiting for Alfred to come back, the real contender, not for this mixed-blood who couldn't throw his combinations, who couldn't walk out of his prison.

But it was Jake sitting in a chair under a single naked bulb.

"I'm back, Jake. I'm ready."

Jake stared right through him as if he were invisible.

Sonny woke up sweating. I don't exist to a dead man.

He borrowed Malik's laptop. Told him he wanted to check out the flesh.

He sent a message to the Warrior

Angel from his private e-mail address, Moscondagabrave@aol.com.

He wrote:

I don't know where to go.

Eight

THE LAND ROVER was back on the highway, heading west, when Starkey spotted flashing police lights in a corner of the rearview mirror. He felt a dry lump rise in his throat. It's finished before it even started, he thought. He imagined pulling off the road, sitting like a child as the cop swaggered over, demanded a license he didn't have, registration and insurance he didn't know where to find. He would have to try very hard not to react to the cop's attitude, remember he was on a Mission for the Creator, that he wasn't here to act out for himself.

"Act out what?" asked PJ. The lump gagged him.

The police lights began to grow in the mirror like poisonous flowers.

He could make a run for it. The Land Rover had some power; he could feel it throb under him like a Thoroughbred stallion that wants to be turned loose. But it probably couldn't outrun a souped-up police cruiser, and even if it could, there would be dozens of cop cars up ahead waiting for him. Planes and helicopters if Stepdad got into the action. Been there, done that.

And there's always a chance of a crack-up in a high-speed chase. I can risk that for myself if the Mission depended on it, but I can't expose a Live One like PJ. The Archies are always hammering us on that. You're down there to save them, not hurt them.

"Who are the Archies?" asked PJ.

The red flower filled the mirror.

"The Archangels are like the elders of the tribe, the chiefs who know almost everything."

"Almost?"

"Only the Creator knows everything."

He brought his foot up slowly on the accelerator.

"Why are you slowing down?"

Sirens.

"Let me do the talking, PJ."

"Please don't call me PJ anymore." Her voice cracked. "That's not me, PJ, I don't want to be that person who can't . . ."

The cop car swept past. He felt his breath

follow it out of his body and down the highway.

" . . . get dressed, who can't get on with her life. My name is Allysse."

He waited until he could breathe again. "You never said anything in Circle."

"I didn't want to get anyone mad at me."

That was pure paranoia, he thought. I wasn't going over the speed limit and it's too early for Mom to have called the cops. He could imagine her still in the store, clerks smelling the limitless credit on her plastic cards, fluttering around as she examined a hundred shirts and ties. Been there, done that, too.

But I'll have to ditch the Rover, jack or hot-wire another car, maybe mix it up with a bus or train. Got to move fast. Ditch PJ, too.

"Ditch me?"

"Find a place to drop you off."

"Why?"

"I've got a job to do, and I can't take you with me."

She snapped open her seat belt. "Then I don't care, drop me off here." She opened the door and started swinging her legs out. He could see the highway flashing past below her feet. Was she testing him, or was she ready to jump?

He imagined her hitting the highway at sixty miles an hour, leaving a trail of blood and hair until she rolled to a stop as a lump of warm roadkill. One way to get rid of her.

Convenient.

But wrong. The Creator would never forgive me.

"Nooooo." He grabbed her arm and pulled her back. It took all his strength to steer and hang on to her. "We'll talk about it. After you close the door."

She closed the door. "Starkey, I'm not going back there. I want to be with you."

"Buckle up." When she did, he said, "I'm not promising to go all the way with you."

"I'm not sure I'm ready for sex, Starkey."

He swallowed the laugh. Dumb but pure. One of the true Live Ones, the people the Band of Angels and the Legion of Evil are fighting over. But I can't lose focus. She is not my Mission, she can only get in the way.

"Okay. Find us a town with a north-south railroad line, rich enough so this baby won't cause attention when we leave it in the parking lot. You really like Allysse?"

"Ally, call me Ally." She laughed and

squeezed his leg so hard, his foot jerked on the pedal and the Rover burst into speed.

He laughed with her, pretended that every-thing was all right now. "But first, Ally, get us some tunes. Driving music. No opera, no gangsta rap. No Locs 'n' Bagels."

"They're over," she said. "Phony interracial group put together by some music company hustlers."

"Awww-right, let's go. We're off to Vegas to save Sonny."

"Sonny the boxer? But didn't he win?"

"He won the fight, but he's lost. I'll explain along the way."

He didn't explain, of course. You only do that when you want to keep Live Ones off bal-ance, when letting them think you are crazy is in the best interests of the Mission. And then there are the times when you need to step out of your undercover clothes and be a Live One yourself. That's very tricky, because you might begin to think there is a crazy side to you after all, and you need to take the pills and listen to the shrinks who will bury it.

"Have you been taking your pills?"

Who am I kidding, how can this work? Live Ones are always trying to control each other. "What's it to you?"

"When you don't, you sort of . . . go away."

"I'm right here."

"You know what I mean. I feel I can't even touch you." Her hand hovered over his leg.

He was going to have to deal with this soon, dump the vehicle and dump her.

The Harley Fat Boy was a hard, intense ride. It took all of Starkey's concentration to keep it moving along the back roads of Indiana and Iowa. Stealing it was easier than steering it. Macho bikers are always leaving their hogs in packs outside bars, keys in the ignition, so sure nobody would dare mess with their rides.

Ally held him tight, murmuring encouragement as he wove through farm traffic and passed tractor trailers on narrow roads. She seemed so unafraid, so sure of him, that he felt clear and powerful, the Warrior Angel at the top of his game, out of reach of the Voices and the powers that changed shapes. His vision was laser sharp, he could see around bends.

Until he lost control on a patch of loose

gravel and spilled out.

They were wearing the helmets the biker had left hanging from the handlebars, and except for bruised shoulders and hips they weren't hurt. But it broke the spell. Suddenly they were both exhausted. They took a room in a cheap motel off the highway, bought a huge bucket of fried chicken and a six-pack of sodas, and took turns soaking in the bathtub before they fell into bed. She was asleep immediately, so he didn't have to deal with the touching thing.

He woke early and booted the laptop. Thank the Creator it hadn't crashed in the crash.

I don't know where to go.

Hot and cold up his spine. It was the message he had been waiting for all his life.

The reply was the message he had been waiting all his life to send.

Dear George Harrison Bayer,
Meet me at the top of the stairs.
Warrior Angel

Nine

THEY WERE YELLING in the living room of the hotel suite for a long time before Sonny woke up. He was dreaming again of Donatelli's Gym. Alfred was leaning against the ropes, watching Sonny spar with himself. Two Sonnys in the ring, unable to slip each other's jabs, unable to mount the combinations to knock each other out, two Sonnys staggering around the ring while Alfred shook his head.

Sonny was sweating when he lurched out of his bedroom.

Hubbard was yelling at Malik and kicking his legs as he scampered around the room whimpering, and Boyd was pleading with him to stop. Hubbard jabbed a thick finger at the laptop, sitting on the floor at a crazy angle. "What's this, what's this?"

"E-mail," wailed Malik.

"I know that, you fool. Tell me how you let

someone from the outside slip messages to Sonny."

Malik whined, "We didn't know—"

"No we, I'm talkin' to you."

"How was I to know?"

"What you supposed to do but know?" Hubbard scooped up the laptop and read, "*Dear George Harrison Bayer, Meet me at the top of the stairs. Warrior Angel.* What's this mean?"

"That was on Sonny's private e-mail. Malik had to . . ." Boyd stopped when he saw Sonny.

Hubbard looked up. "What's this about, Sonny?"

"You reading my mail?" He tried to sound angry to cover his excitement. The path was suddenly clear.

"Trying to protect you," shouted Hubbard. He dropped the laptop on the carpet. Malik flinched. Hubbard advanced on Sonny, jabbing his finger. "Who this Warrior Angel?"

"My private mail?"

"Nothing private from us."

"Even his mind?" asked Dr. Gould. No one had noticed him come into the room.

In a moment of dead silence everyone froze. Sonny almost laughed. Hubbard's big mouth hung open like a steam shovel. Boyd and Malik were crouched at his knees.

Finally, Hubbard said, "What you want?"

"Sonny and I have an appointment."

"Been canceled. Send me your bill," said Hubbard.

"Sonny?" Dr. Gould raised his eyebrows.

This was no time to take a stand against Hubbard, Sonny thought. Fighter has to know when to attack, when to retreat, when to clinch. Alfred told me that once. Know what I've got to do now. Warrior Angel showed me the way.

When Sonny shook his head, Dr. Gould pulled a business card out of a small leather case and handed it to Sonny. "If you ever want to call me . . ."

"He won't." Hubbard snatched the card out of Sonny's hand, tore it in half, and let the two pieces flutter to the ground. "He been shrunk enough. Good-bye."

Dr. Gould waited a beat, looking at Sonny. When there was no response, he said, "Good luck, Sonny," and walked out.

"Man, you nailed that sucka, Elston," said Malik, "you—"

"Shut up. Sonny—who this Warrior Angel?"

73

"Some fan, I guess."

"You give him a private e-mail?" Hubbard was advancing again.

Sonny remembered a moment late one night in the latrine at Whitmore, the X-Men advancing on him, demanding he join their gang. He'd stood up then, and ended up stabbed on the white tile floor. Be cool, Sonny. Swallow the monster down.

Sonny shrugged.

Malik said, "Must be a hacker, right? Hacked in."

Hubbard didn't look convinced. "Fight in less than five weeks, Sonny. No time for dee-stractions. You got to focus, get your game back. You got to be like a monk."

Sonny thought, Like a prisoner, but didn't say anything.

"So. No more e-mail, he-mail, she-mail, just rest and train," said Hubbard. "Any video games you want, movies, CDs, you just tell Boyd or Malik. Booked a gym across town, no one bother us, start running tomorrow morning. Okay?"

Boyd and Malik nodded like bobblehead dolls.

Hubbard pointed down at the laptop. "Lose it."

"Need it for my work," squeaked Malik.

Hubbard mimicked him. "Need it for my work." He stomped on the laptop, driving the heels of his boots into the screen until it cracked. "Your work is what I tell you to do."

Hubbard picked up the computer and hurled it against the wall so hard, it gouged out a chunk. He marched out of the room and slammed the door. Sonny could hear him shouting at the guards in the hallway that there were terrorists out to get Sonny, to shoot on sight.

Malik was down on his knees, cradling the broken laptop like a doll. "Why he have to—"

"We'll get another one," said Boyd. He put his hand on Malik's shoulder.

Sonny edged past them, scooped up the two pieces of Dr. Gould's torn business card, and slipped back into his bedroom. Got to think.

He was twenty stories up. The windows were bolted shut. Think. Marty always said, Sonny's not as dumb as he looks. Miss that fat owl. Got to get out of here. Even if I could punch my way off the floor through the guards outside, they'd stop the elevators or nail me in the lobby.

Running Braves could think.

So think.

He called room service, ordered enormous meals for three.

He took his time showering, dressing. The wallet he had locked in the room safe before the fight was still there, with eighteen hundred dollars and his credit cards. He was ready by the time the food arrived, a bathrobe over his clothes.

"Hey, Sonny, you order this?" Boyd was at the door. Malik was in a corner, still mourning over his laptop.

"Figured you guys could use a good meal. Send mine in. I want to eat in bed."

When the room service waiter in his Vegas-style Arabian robe and hood rolled the food cart in, Sonny closed the door behind him and pressed a roll of cash into his hand. "I need your uniform and twenty minutes."

The waiter understood right away. "It's my job, Sonny. But you could tie me up."

The best they could find were the long laces on old boxing shoes to tie the waiter's ankles and wrists behind him. Just before Sonny taped his mouth shut, the waiter said, "Good luck, champ."

Malik and Boyd were pigging out and didn't look up as Sonny rolled the empty food cart out of the suite. In the hall one of the guards said, "Nothing for us?" but Sonny kept his head down and deep inside the hood. The service elevator was empty. He left the cart in the basement, stripped off the flowing robe in the parking lot. The boxing ring and the chairs were gone. Like the fight had never happened. Okay with me.

He walked to another hotel before he hailed a cab. With his ponytail tucked into a baseball cap and his hand on his face, no one recognized him at the airport. He'd catch an overnight flight to New York. George Harrison Bayer's credit card wouldn't send up any red flags for a while. Sleep on the plane, cab to Harlem, then back up to the top of the stairs and the Warrior Angel.

Ten

ALLY WANTED TO KNOW why they were heading east now, where they were going.

"I told you, to save Sonny."

"That's what, not where." There was a sharpness in her voice he hadn't heard before.

The sharpness reminded him of the razor blade in the binding of the book. Once, he had sat on his bed and drawn the edge along his wrist, then across his throat, leaving red trails but not breaking the skin. Then he'd opened his shirt and pressed one pointy corner against the left side of his chest where he thought his heart might be. That had left a red pinprick mark.

He had felt good, in control, knowing that if the Voices ever became unbearable, he could cut them off forever.

"Cut what off?"

"Too many questions." It came out more harshly than he intended, but it shut her up.

Driving through Pennsylvania in the Neon

he had hot-wired in the motel parking lot, he relaxed. The highway was wide, the farms on either side green. Ally found a radio station that played heavy metal. The music had a throbbing beat that kept the Voices out of his head.

"I used to play the violin," said Ally.

"No kidding. You ever get those red hickeys on your neck?"

"All the time. How'd you know about that?"

"There was a girl in my class, they always made fun of her. Said she was making out, when all she did was practice."

"That was me," said Ally. She laughed. She started telling a story about how much she loved playing in her junior high school orchestra, being a part of the music, but her voice faded as he remembered how that red spot on the girl's neck had scared him. He had thought it was the mark of the devil. He couldn't keep his eyes off it. Finally he'd tried to rub it off her. That was the first time they sent him to the hospital.

"Hospital?"

He switched gears. "Alfred went into the hospital after Sonny won the title. He's a paraplegic, got shot in the spine. Then Jake got sick and died, and things turned bad for Sonny. All the important people in his life disappeared. He became vulnerable to Hubbard."

"I was in the middle of telling you a story." She sounded annoyed. Her mouth snapped shut.

She is going to be a problem, he thought, making an effort to keep the thought inside his head. Got to get rid of her now. He spotted a sign for a big truck stop in ten miles. Food, rooms, showers. It was a sign from Upstairs.

Starkey had the skateboard dream. No surprise. During a Mission you always have dreams that are really messages from the Archies. One of the main ways they communicate. But you have to decode the dreams, figure them out.

The skateboard dream began at the skate park, Sonny wowing the crowd on the half pipe, popping Ollies, and riding the lip and coming closer to a double McSick than anybody in town ever dreamed of.

Most of the kids in town are wearing the same colors and brand of helmet and elbow and knee pads that he's wearing. Red and black. Sonny's the champ, a hero.

And then Starkey sweeps by, no helmet or pads, in his blue-and-white Skate and Die T-shirt, and Sonny sees him and knows what he has to do, and he comes down the ramp and trails him back to the old mill on the edge of town. All the kids follow, they try to talk to Sonny, but he is shaking his head and stripping off the helmet and pads, no street skater is going to show him up. The champ, the golden boy, the favored one.

The caretaker, the guy who watches the mill at night, comes out, shakes his head, and goes back into his dusty little room.

Starkey starts slow and easy, gliding along the stone landings, then down the concrete steps on the side of the old mill. Sonny can do that, he's smiling, the crowd is all jiggly, clapping for him. Starkey vaults over the steel railing a couple of times, landing back on the board, spinning once, and Sonny is still keeping up with him.

Then Starkey takes him to the rim, a ledge of concrete maybe six inches wide that runs along the edge of an old road. On the other side of the rim is a long drop into acres of rusted machinery, jagged, all the old mill equipment that got thrown out over the years, that the town hasn't yet found the money to haul away. A garden of spears.

Starkey starts slow again, a few easy Ollies, a half spin that has him moving backward, another half spin that has him facing front, a full spin off the board, follow the leader, Sonny, and now the crowd is getting nervous but Sonny is only thinking about follow the leader so he can be leader again, and Starkey takes the board to the lips of the rim, first on the road side, then on the jagged-machinery side, back and forth, two wheels whining at a time, and he stamps on the tail as he goes up and comes down on the nose, one foot, no one's ever seen this before, and suddenly he wants to stop, tell Sonny not to do this, but his tongue is stuck to the roof of his mouth and everyone's screaming as Sonny falls, head over board, into the rusty steel jungle below.

Eleven

SONNY REMEMBERED the first time he had pounded up the narrow, twisting stairs of Donatelli's Gym, at midnight, taking them two at a time, not waiting for his eyes to adjust to the darkness. He threw open the creaky old door marked GYM and Alfred Brooks was waiting for him, sitting under a single naked light bulb. When Alfred said, "What took you so long, young gentleman?" he suddenly felt safe. For the first time, he felt he had a future.

Now he took the steps slowly, one by one, feeling each sag under his boots, complain in a woody screech. You really want to do this, Sonny? Got to. Want to? No choice. He pushed open the door.

Same old gym, worn and dirty, stinking of sweat and liniment and the bleach that could never erase all the blood from the wooden floor. Curling on the walls were old fight posters and old signs, NO SPITTING IN THE GYM, and PAY DUES

83

THE FIRST OF THE MONTH, EVERY MONTH. The late-afternoon sun slanting through the filthy windows trapped tornados of dust motes in tubes of golden light. Buzzers and bells counted off three-minute rounds and one-minute rest periods.

Boxers skipped rope, shadowboxed, slugged the heavy bags, and peppered the light bags while trainers watched them or yelled at them or gossiped with each other as if the boxers didn't exist. He recognized most of them. Old Dave (The Fave) Reynolds, still lumbering after a heavyweight title shot, was up in the ring sparring with a younger, quicker fighter, who had two guys in suits shouting advice up to him. Guess which one's getting the next title shot.

The owner, Henry Johnson, tall and skinny, wearing his usual white shirt and tie, limped briskly around the big room, pulling on his little gray beard, spraying advice, snapping orders, showing a young fighter how to turn his fist on the jab, growling at a kid to pass around the water bottles. Johnson didn't miss a thing.

"What you want?" said Johnson.

The room dropped dead. The shouts, the

thump of the bags, the patter of feet, suddenly stopped. Everybody was looking at Sonny, ignoring the buzzers and bells.

Johnson started moving toward him, dragging his leg. "This is no Hollywood gym, this is no Wall Street health club, so what you doing here?"

It was a real question. Johnson stared at him stone-faced, waiting for the answer. Sunny choked it out. "Need a place to train."

"You're not welcome here no more."

A fat man hustled up, wiping his sweating moon face. "Henry, this man is heavyweight champion of the world. You got to respect the title, least hear him out."

"Don't got to do anything, Horace. This my place." Johnson looked stern. "What do you think Mr. Donatelli would say?"

"That was a different time," said Horace. Sonny felt grateful. He remembered the fat man, a former fighter who owned a ribs restaurant called Jelly Belly's. He had eaten there with Alfred and Johnson.

"I believe in second chances, third chances," said Johnson. "But I don't think this boy has earned his."

"Sonny." The Fave was pulling off his head-guard, leaning over the ropes. "Talk to us, man, what happened to you? Why'd you walk on everybody?"

He hated the way they were all looking at him, making him feel small, pushing him under-water. He remembered nights fighting smokers in hillbilly towns when the hatred of the cracker crowds slapped his body with a fine cold spray that gave the monster strength. Where is the monster now?

"We'll listen to you, Sonny," said Horace.

"Talk fast," said Johnson. "After you walked out on us, stayed with Hubbard, why should we give you the time of day?"

Sonny had no answer. He wasn't going to beg.

"That's a no-brainer."

A voice from the doorway, a voice Sonny had never heard before, high and hard and clear, knifed through the dusty murk of the gym. "He put this dump on the map, and you owe him one."

Johnson's mouth fell open. "What?"

"You heard me." A tall, skinny teenaged boy was marching toward the ring, his long dark hair flopping over his pale face. "Sonny is going through a personal crisis, and if you can't see that, Mr. Johnson, you're not the crippled little kid who made himself the best trainer in the business."

Sonny lost his breath. His chest vibrated as if his lungs had become wings beating against the insides of his ribs. The wings of the Hawk. How long since he had felt that spirit?

"Who are you?" asked Johnson.

"My name is Starkey Brant, and I've come to help you get Sonny ready for the title fight."

"Help me?" Johnson's voice squeaked with outrage.

I know this boy, Sonny thought.

"I'll take my orders from you, Mr. Johnson, but I know you agree we need to get back to basics. Dust off Rocky—"

"Who are you?" asked Johnson.

"—and we'll need to work on his head."

"I said, who are you?"

"It's very complicated, but for now consider me your assistant trainer."

"Consider you crazy." Johnson was shaking his head. "You know this boy, Sonny?"

"He's come to save me," said Sonny. He was

87

laughing, suddenly feeling safe here again, with a future.

"Is he crazy?" said Johnson.

"He's the Warrior Angel," said Sonny.

It took another hour of standing around, Johnson muttering while Horace and the Fave pleaded with him to give Sonny a chance. Starkey sponged off Rocky and hung it up in a corner. The other boxers went back to work, but they kept glancing over their shoulders. Sonny sensed that they liked the idea of the heavyweight champ back training at Donatelli's, but they didn't want Johnson to make it too easy on him. He'd walked out on them once. Why wouldn't he do it again?

"If Alfred was feeling better, I'd let him make the decision," said Johnson. "Don't want to bother him. You got some sort of plan?"

Just to be here, thought Sonny.

"Of course," said Starkey. Where did this kid get his confidence? "Sonny's going to sleep here, help keep the place up, just like he did when he was starting. He has to prove his sincerity."

Johnson blinked. "That right, Sonny?"

88

Sonny nodded.

Johnson asked, "What about you?"

Before Starkey could answer, Sonny said, "He stays here too."

Johnson took a step back and looked him over. "Never seen this before," he muttered, and Sonny knew everything was going to be all right.

Twelve

I T WAS MORE THAN Starkey had ever imagined, just the two of them, sitting on ring stools at a spindly card table, under a single naked bulb in the middle of the gym. They were eating barbecued ribs that Horace had sent over from his restaurant. Sonny ate the ribs carefully, turning them almost delicately in his big hands as he nibbled around the bone. Starkey tried to copy Sonny, but his fingers were not as nimble and the ribs slipped in his hands.

So close to Sonny that he had to remember to breathe. He tried not to stare. Sonny's face seemed softer than in the poster on Starkey's bedroom wall, his jawline not so bony. There were small scars around his eyebrows and mouth. But his eyes were as deep and dark as they were in pictures. The teeth picking at the meat on the ribs were large and white. His knuckles were scuffed.

There were a million questions he wanted to

ask, but Sonny seemed closed up into himself, focused on eating. Athletes are like that, Starkey remembered reading somewhere, able to zone in on whatever they were doing and shut out distractions. They miss a lot, but they get the job done. A Warrior Angel is a kind of athlete.

"So what's a Warrior Angel?" The rib, dripping sauce, was poised at Sonny's lips.

Thinking out loud again, Starkey. Now you better think fast. Another defining moment. But this may not be the time to go for it. Be cool, be steady.

"We help people."

"How?"

"Support them in their strengths, protect them from their weaknesses."

"What's that mean?" Sonny's brow was wrinkled. He looked like he wanted a real answer.

"If you've got a killer left hook, learn how to use it even more effectively. If your chin's weak, learn how to protect it."

"Trainers do that."

"Right. Now take that beyond boxing, to the whole person." Starkey thought, Easy here, don't want to spook him. "Say you're good at

91

setting goals and never quitting till you get there. It's important that you set the right goals or you'll be off wandering on worthless journeys. Say you've got a tendency to be negative. You need to be reminded of positive things."

Sonny nodded and went back to the rib.

Well done, Starkey. When you are cool, you are in control. Could have babbled on and blown it. But the fistful of pills he had swiped from the Family Place wouldn't last forever, even at the half dosage he was taking. To stretch it out I'll have to cut back to a quarter dose soon. Then the Voices will start drifting back. Got to get the job done before I run out.

Sonny glanced up. "What job?"

"Getting you ready for The Wall."

Sonny seemed to like that. "You told Johnson you had a plan."

"Mind and body. Both have to be in better shape. For starters, this is the last dinner of ribs till after the fight." Starkey loved the easy authority in his voice. The Archies would be proud. "The Wall wasn't prepared for you last time, took you lightly. He won't make that mistake again."

"It was a war," said Sonny. He put down a

half-eaten rib and wiped his mouth. "I was piss-
ing blood and seeing double for a week. And I
was ready last time."

"Not so ready," said Starkey. "You were dis-
tracted. All the stuff on the Reservation.
Remember, somebody tried to shoot you. That
can take you out of the zone."

Sonny nodded. He was listening!

Starkey felt an electric surge. He was getting through. "Rocky'll get your rhythms and
combinations back, and we'll work on focusing
your head. Turn on the lights. Clear out the
fog."

"You think I'm a head case?"

Careful, Starkey. "I think you let yourself get
down, the same way you let your conditioning
slip."

Sonny nodded. "I felt like I was digging a
hole, couldn't stop digging the hole, just getting
deeper and deeper in."

"But you jumped out, Sonny." Starkey swallowed his excitement. All the years of therapy
paying off—I should be a shrink. "You shook
loose of Hubbard, came back here."

"You helped me do that."

Starkey felt almost dizzy with the intensity

of Sonny's stare. They were eye locked, nothing else happening in the world but the energy flowing between them.

Suddenly Sonny stood up, so quickly the stool toppled over behind him and ribs scattered on the table. Steel shutters snapped down over his eyes. "Better get some sleep." He marched across the gym and piled three mats in a corner. He yanked off his running shoes.

"There's a couch in Johnson's office," he said. "Up at six."

He wrapped a big towel around himself and sank to the mats. He pulled his knees to his chest and was asleep before Starkey pulled the light cord.

The couch was old and stained and smelly, there were hard spots and soft spots, and it took Starkey a while to burrow his body into a groove. But he was too excited to sleep right away. He had made the connection. Sonny was listening to him. And he'd stayed cool.

But Sonny was going to be tough. The way he had suddenly jumped up to end the conversation. A warning bell had gone off in his head when he had felt Starkey getting too close. Was it about accepting help from someone else?

Maybe he had a fear of becoming vulnerable to someone else, and then abandoned, the way his mother had dumped him on the Res for months at a time.

Maybe that's too simple, the quickie, Family Circle Jerk explanation. I'll need to get to the real Sonny. And then maybe he'll open up so I can save him.

I'll have to take it easy bringing him to that point. Starkey remembered once going fishing with Stepdad, who kept lecturing him to reel in firmly but slowly or the fish would snap the line and swim away. He'd listened to what Stepdad said and kept jerking on the rod all day long so the fish could break away to freedom.

He'd have to play Sonny slowly to bring him into the boat.

After a while the lights of a pink dawn bled through the dusty windows of Donatelli's Gym. On the Harlem street below, a garbage truck ground up metal to a chorus of drunks.

Sonny kicked over a metal bucket. "Let's go, Warrior Angel."

Through gummy eyelashes Starkey saw the clock over Johnson's desk. It was just five-thirty. He staggered out and watched Sonny wash his face and head in a mop sink, then shake off the water like a dog.

"We'll get coffee and oranges at Kim's."

"Not even six," said Starkey.

"Best time to run, before the car fumes."

"You want me to run with you?" Maybe I can do it, he thought. I wasn't kicked off the cross-country team for being too slow.

"You're on the bike."

Thirteen

ONCE SONNY FELT the heat rising up his legs, the blood running free through loosening muscles, he could imagine toxins draining out of his body and the darkness slipping out of his mind. He always felt better when he was running, best of all on a crisp morning when the run was the start of a training day. He had a plan, he was in control. He knew what he was doing.

He could hear Starkey, hunched under his backpack, wheezing along behind him on the battered old gym bike, towels and water bottles in the basket, squeaking along a slalom course of garbage and broken bottles and ruptured concrete on the fifteen blocks down to Central Park. His steering was a little erratic, but he was pedaling steadily enough to keep up.

Been a while since I had someone I liked on the chase bike behind me, he thought. A long time since I opened up the way I did last night.

Warrior Angel? More like the president of the Sonny Bear Fan Club. That's cool. Just be careful. These touchy-feely types like to get into your head, and once they get in, they're hard to get out. They want to wake up all the sleeping dogs, make you think about all the things you don't want to think about.

He thought about Alfred. Be hard to just pick up the phone and call him.

The sounds of the city faded as they moved deeper into the park. The horns and the sirens and the car alarms grew distant. There were moments he could imagine himself back on the Res. When Jake was alive.

Someone else he didn't want to think about.

"Angel!" He waved Starkey alongside and grabbed a plastic water bottle out of the bike basket. "How you doing?"

"Fine," Starkey gasped. Sonny lifted the bottle to hide his grin. "How many . . . miles . . . you run?"

"Don't know. Forty-five minutes good, like a twelve-round fight. You need to wear that backpack?"

"I do." He said it sharply, a flicker of panic in his eyes.

Sonny shrugged, then tossed the bottle back into the basket and surged ahead.

After breakfast Sonny trained hard for two hours, finishing up in a three-round sparring session with Cobra Rasheed, a hard-punching light heavyweight. Cobra was training for a ten-rounder on the Hall undercard. If he won, he could move up in the rankings. If he won and looked good, he might even get a shot at the title.

Cobra had a lot of attitude, which was okay with Sonny, but he was trying to show off by scoring on Sonny, which was not okay. He knew Sonny wouldn't unload on him. It wouldn't look right, the champ with a thirty-pound weight advantage. So Cobra played the baby-bully game. He was supposed to give Sonny a speed workout, help him ratchet up his quickness to stay away from the slow but heavy-hitting Hall. But he moved in to punch, popping a short right that snapped Sonny's head back and pummeling Sonny's ribs in a clinch. Sonny was able to smother the body shots by clamping his arms over Cobra's and pulling him in close.

"You okay, champ?" Cobra sneered.

Sonny shoved him away.

At the bell Johnson said, "This for speed-work, Rasheed. Just box, don't bang."

Cobra snickered. "Sor-reee. Didn't mean to hurt the champ." He winked at his trainers, who shook their heads in warning.

Sonny felt an old stirring, and it felt good. Was the monster coming back? Been missing that old slugger. The Warrior Angel had been right to get him back to Donatelli's.

Cobra swaggered out for the last round flat-footed, ready to mix it up. But Sonny danced away, batting aside his jabs, skipping in and out of range until Cobra dropped his hands and snarled, "Someday this be for real." His corner-men crowed at that, and Johnson shook his head. Sonny just kept moving until the bell rang, but he felt frustrated. He would have liked to rattle Cobra's cage.

"Hands too slow," said Johnson, toweling him off. "Got to snap those jabs out."

"I'll get on Rocky."

"Be with you in a—"

"Let's see what the Angel got."

Johnson looked dubious, but he shrugged.

Starkey looked panicky at first, staring at

the life-sized dummy. From forehead to waist its canvas skin was divided into numbered sections. The point of Rocky's chin was marked 1. Seven was his right eye, 8 was his left. His nose was 3. The middle of his belly was 17.

Starkey started slow, his calls tentative. "Jab . . . one. Jab . . . seven. Hook . . . nine."

Sonny felt impatient but wanted to give him a chance. It took a few minutes for Starkey to warm up, but then the pace picked up. "Jab, seven, jab, nine, right, thirteen."

Soon there was a logic to the calls, combinations that started with crisp jabs to put an opponent off balance, body shots to drive him back to the ropes, hooks to the head to put him away. The kid knew something about boxing.

Sonny felt himself absorbed into the rhythms of the three-round flurries. He nodded encouragement at Starkey during the one-minute rests. "Way to go . . . pick it up."

After six rounds Johnson said, "Enough for today."

Sonny, breathing hard, dropped his arms and stepped back. For the first time, he noticed that trainers and boxers had formed a semicircle behind him. Someone shouted, "Way to go, champ."

Sonny felt good. He was back.

Cobra pushed out of the crowd, and said, "Dummy don't have no arms to hit back."

Starkey said, "You're the dummy *with* arms."

Laughter rippled through the gym. Cobra closed his fists, took a breath. He said to Sonny, "Your little brother got a big mouth."

Sonny glanced at Starkey, who looked proud of himself. *You're the dummy with arms* was a line Marty Witherspoon had once used, Sonny remembered. It was in the book. So was a lot of information about Rocky, including one entire chapter on how to use the dummy to practice your offensive attack.

So what, he's read the book. Still, something felt a little creepy.

Fourteen

THAT NIGHT, WHILE they were cleaning up, Kim brought up Styrofoam containers packed with chicken, rice and beans, and salad from his takeout table. He fussed as he arranged the food on the table and left beaming as they dug in.

Sonny seemed in a good mood, relaxed. He hummed over the food before he brought it to his mouth.

"You've got friends," said Starkey.

"Kim liked Jake. Reminded him of his grandfather back in Korea."

"You miss Jake?"

Sonny shrugged.

"What about Alfred?"

"Got to call him one of these days."

Starkey felt a pinprick of anxiety. Sonny wants to see Alfred. Be careful, Starkey. Don't forget that the Mission comes first. Saving Sonny, helping him reclaim his soul from the dark forces, means getting him back with his old friends. You have to guard against your own feelings. Warrior Angels must not be jealous of relationships among Live Ones.

Keep talking, don't react.

"One thing I don't get."

Sonny laughed. "Lucky, only one thing."

"Champs have people around them, body-guards, entourages, posses to hang out with and do stuff."

"You're my posse."

"I'm serious."

"I know how to tape my own hands if I have to," said Sonny.

"What's that mean?"

"You can't depend on people." He made it sound like the slamming of a door.

When the classic-rock station Sonny had tuned in played a Beatles song, Starkey tried again.

"Beatles," said Starkey. "Do you like being named after a Beatle?"

Sonny shrugged. When he doesn't feel like talking, Starkey thought, he just locks up. That was in The Book, too.

Sonny glanced over a drumstick. "You

read the book?"

Here we go again, the out-loud problem.

"I read the entire book six times," said Starkey. "Some parts I read a dozen times. I underlined the Running Braves stuff." He saw that Sonny's eyes were narrowing, his mouth tightening into a hard line, and he tried to stop but couldn't.

"The Warrior Angels are sort of like the Running Braves. You try to help your people too."

"My people?"

"The Moscondaga Nation."

Sonny snorted. "Give me a break. Moscondaga Nation's a joke. They spend most of their time fighting with each other. The old-fashioned Indians are waiting for the buffalo to come back and for the white man to go back to Europe. The new-fashioned ones are looking to sell out to the mob so they can get rich on a casino."

"And you tried to bring them together."

"Both sides treated me like a cracker until I was champ."

"So you feel more white than Indian?"

"White people treated me like a Redskin

until I got to be champ. That's why the title's crap too. Doesn't mean anything except money. And Hubbard steals most of it."

"So why are you fighting?"

"You got a better job for a mixed-blood high school dropout?" He glared at Starkey. "Maybe president of a dot-com?"

Starkey decided to take a chance, see if Sonny had a sense of humor. "Sure. We'll call it Dot Combinations. It's just what you need."

It took Sonny a beat to realize Starkey was making a joke, and another beat to get the joke, but he laughed and reached out to cuff him lightly on the shoulder. "That's a good one. Got to tell Marty." He scowled. "Someday."

Starkey couldn't control the little jolts, first of delight, then jealousy. Martin Malcolm Witherspoon, author of The Tomahawk Kid, was another friend who could be used for the Mission. Mr. Johnson, Alfred, Martin, one by one, bring them back to help save Sonny.

And squeeze you out, whispered a Voice.

Stay cool. Focus.

He thought of the dog-eared copy of The Book in his backpack. "I know some of that book by heart. 'The best of them could smell the

106

breath of their prey. . . .'"

Sonny growled, deep in his throat.

He couldn't help himself—he plunged on. "Your great-grandfather was the last of the Running Braves; he was murdered by—"

WHAP! Sonny's big hand smacked the spindly table so hard that rice and beans jumped out of the Styrofoam boxes. "No Redskin crap."

"Not crap, it's—"

"That's where you got the idea for Warrior Angels? From the book?"

Starkey felt as though he'd been punched in the stomach, the breath wheezing out of him. "You . . . you think I made it up?"

"Somebody made up the Running Braves, right?"

"But they existed," said Starkey. "Everything was made up by somebody. And the Creator made up everybody."

Sonny shook his head. "You sound like Jake. So, where you from?"

"North of here." Starkey jerked a thumb toward Upstairs. It was the first personal question Sonny had asked, and he didn't want to scare him.

"You a runaway?" Sonny didn't look concerned when Starkey nodded. "What you running from?"

"I was in a . . . group home. For kids having problems."

"What's your problem?"

Take a chance, tell him the truth. Well, one true story of many. "I was in boarding school and I pulled down the water tower behind the dorm." Don't mention that the Voices had told him that the water was poisoned. When he tried to warn the headmaster, he wouldn't listen and the other kids made fun of him, beat him up.

"How'd you do it?"

"Middle of the night, I looped cables around the wooden stilts that held up the tower and I attached them to the tow hook of the maintenance truck." Starkey was thrilled with Sonny's rapt attention. "I was in first gear when the stilts cracked, then I shifted to third and gunned the motor. Pulled it right down behind me."

"Lucky you didn't drown."

Don't tell him you were prepared to drown to save the school from the poisoned water. That's what Warrior Angels do. We sacrifice ourselves when there's no other way to complete our Mission. "Turned out there was no water in the tank."

"Did you know that?"

"You think I'm that crazy?" He made himself laugh. Don't tell him how surprised you were to find out the tank was dry. It had been a test from the Creator.

"What kind of test?"

"A test for my stepdad's lawyers. Cost him plenty to keep me out of jail. I was expelled and they sent me to the Family Place." Was it the Family Place or some other place? He suddenly couldn't remember. There had been so many places. None of them had meant anything until he found The Book, and discovered Sonny and his true Mission.

"The Family Place?" Was Sonny really interested or was he trying to trip me up?

"The group home. I eloped."

"Eloped?"

"That's what they call it when you run away from a loony bin, an elopement."

Sonny nodded. "They looking for you, your folks, cops?"

Starkey looked at him warily. "Probably. Does that make you nervous?"

Sonny smiled. It was the first time Starkey had seen him really smile. He even had dimples. "Nervous? You came to save me, right?"

He felt pure joy surge through his body.

The next day a TV crew showed up to shoot Sonny boxing Rocky.

"You want me to call the shots?" asked Starkey.

"You think you should be on TV?"

The Voices snickered. He doesn't really want you.

"Sure I do," whispered Sonny. "But people aren't supposed to know where you eloped to."

"No problem," said Starkey, relieved.

"Let's do it," said Sonny.

"Jab, two," said Starkey, trying to sound crisp as Sonny's left snapped out into the dummy's mouth. "Jab, seven. Right, four. Hook, nine."

He forced his mind into a laser beam, thinking through the combinations, a jab, sometimes three to set up the big punch, a straight right or a hook, then quickly follow with another punisher or shake up the rhythm with another jab. He could see Sonny was getting into it, appreciating that he wasn't just calling out shots, he had a plan, the Warrior Angel knew what he was doing.

"Jab, seven, nine. Right, four. Hook, thirteen."

Someone rang a bell and Sonny ended with a flurry of belly punches, then threw up his arms. The fighters and trainers applauded and whistled.

"You got enough?" said Johnson. "This is a workplace."

"We're good," said Dick, a silver-haired sportscaster Starkey had seen on ESPN. "Quick interview with the champ and we're out of here."

Johnson grumbled and shooed the boxers and trainers back to work. While his crew set up for the interview, Sonny asked, "How'd you know I was here?"

"Little bird," said Dick. "Actually a big one. I was eating at Jelly Belly's. What about Hubbard? Don't you have a contract?"

"He'll get his cut, all he cares about," said Sonny.

"When he sees this, he'll be on the next plane," said Dick.

"I'm a free man," said Sonny. "I'll tell him I'm back with Henry Johnson. And my little brother here."

This time the joy made Starkey dizzy.

They watched the news while they ate spaghetti with meatballs and a salad, a gift from the Italian restaurant up the street. No question the word was out that Sonny was back. People dropped by to watch him train. Sonny seemed cool about the attention. Starkey thought he accepted it as his due. He wondered how long before other people would start getting between Sonny and him, how long before the private dinners would be over, before Sonny would be staying somewhere else. Would there be time to complete his Mission?

The anchor introduced an exclusive on the sports report.

Dick's face filled the screen. "If, as I did, you wondered where the heavyweight champion of the world, Sonny Bear, disappeared to after that last stinker in Vegas, here's some good news for a change. He's back in his home gym in Harlem and back to basics, preparing for his rematch with the ex-champ Floyd (The Wall) Hall."

As Rocky appeared on the screen, Dick said, "That's not just any dummy Sonny Bear's beating up, that's Rocky, the target of thousands of his training punches over the years."

On-screen, Sonny began hammering Rocky as Starkey called out the punches off camera.

The Voices whispered, Sonny told Dick to keep you hidden so he can get rid of you later.

The camera pulled back to show Starkey at Sonny's side. Dick said, "That's Sonny's young assistant trainer, calling the punches."

Sonny elbowed him. "Assistant trainer."

The Voices again: Sonny told Dick to put you on TV so Stepdad'll know where to find you.

The broadcast cut to Dick interviewing Sonny.

"What happened to you in Vegas?"

"I was flat. Couldn't get off."

"We've known each other awhile, Sonny. That wasn't you. There were rumors that you were seeing a psychotherapist."

"Do I look crazy to you?" snapped Sonny.

"Hostile, just hostile," said Dick, smiling. "And that's your job."

The broadcast cut to the anchors, chuckling. One of them said, "Maybe you have to be a little crazy to fight the Wall."

Starkey thought, They're always doing that. "What?"

"Jokes. About being crazy."

Sonny shrugged and kept eating.

"Never bother you?" said Starkey.

"Might, if I was crazy." Sonny thumbed the remote.

The Voices whispered, He thinks you're crazy.

Starkey struggled to keep control, to squeeze the Voices out. A quarter dosage isn't enough. Finally he said, "What . . . doooooo you meannnnnn?"

"You okay?" Sonny's face lengthened, his eyes turned red. He hit the mute button on the TV. "Man, you sound weird. You doing any-thing?"

Starkey tried to answer but nothing was coming out that he could understand. He narrowed his mind, focused, pushed the Voices to the nooks and crannies of his skull. It was exhausting, but it was working. Slowly he found a clear channel to think and then speak.

"I'm okay." He tried to smile. "Better not have dope. Not when Alfred comes around."

Sonny's body jerked. "Alfred's coming around?"

Starkey felt the clear channel vibrating. Don't want to lose this moment. "He's waiting for your call."

"You don't even know him."

I know you all from The Book, Starkey wanted to say, but he said, "Alfred knows you're here. Johnson would have told him. But he can't call you because you walked out on him. You have to make the call."

Sonny shrugged.

"Yooooou heeearrrr meeeeeee?" Starkey took deep breaths, but the gym floor wouldn't stop rippling, the heavy bags were swaying in a cold wind up from Hell, and the Voices were back now and they wouldn't quit anymore tonight.

Sonny stood up. "I'll think about it."

They cleaned up silently. Sonny was back inside himself. Did I drive him there? But I had to. Don't have much time left to save him. Not unless I can get more meds. I had to go for it. Can't read him right now. Is he thinking about calling Alfred? Or is he just shutting me out for going too far too fast, blowing the Mission?

115

Before he tried to sleep, Starkey checked his backpack. Laptop, red cap, The Book. He fingered the ridge in the binding over the razor blade.

Fifteen

LFRED'S WIFE, LENA, was waiting for Sonny at the railroad station. He felt his nervousness drain away when she hugged him and said, "He was so happy you called."

The familiar white HandiVan was out in the parking lot. "How is he?"

"Good days and bad days. He keeps getting these infections. They can knock him down for a week. But he bounces back—you know Alfred."

Alfred was in the driver's seat. He was thinner than Sonny remembered, dark circles around his eyes. A year ago he would never have waited in the car, no matter how hard it was to climb out and into his wheelchair. He must be in a lot of pain.

Lena opened the front passenger door and pushed Sonny forward. All he could think of to say as he climbed in was "Alfred."

Alfred glanced casually over to him and

117

said, "You hungry, young gentleman?" as if they were picking up a recent conversation. They hadn't seen each other in months. The van was moving before Lena had shut her door.

"Sure." He relaxed into the seat. Alfred was going to make it easy, leave the past alone.

"Lena's made some of that sesame chicken you like." Alfred poked a button on his CD player. Old rock music poured out. Sonny could tell he didn't want to talk right now. Fine.

"Where are you living?" Lena leaned over from the backseat.

"The gym."

"Want to stay with us for a few days? Girls be thrilled."

Sonny peeked at Alfred out of the corner of his eye. He was staring straight ahead. Lena must be talking for him, too. Sonny felt his neck muscles soften and relax. "Don't have clothes or—"

"We didn't throw your stuff out," said Alfred. "Yet."

They all laughed.

The house looked the same, a two-story white box on a quiet, shady street of two-story white boxes. Alfred had grown up in Harlem and wanted his kids to grow up in the suburbs. Little lawn out front, big backyard with grill and stone patio. Sonny had set the stones of the patio one weekend. It seemed like a long time ago. Two years?

Tamika and Lysa came home from school just as Sonny and Alfred settled in the den to talk. They burst in, squealing, and began hugging Sonny and throwing mock punches at his jaw. He got up and sparred with them until Lena dragged them out.

"You gonna be ready for the Wall?"

"I'll be there."

"Not my question."

Sonny shrugged. "Should be in shape. But I don't know what happened with Crockett."

"Never saw you like that. Fighting in slow motion."

"Felt like I was drugged."

"Looked like you didn't want to be there," said Alfred. "Hubbard call you?"

"Doesn't know where I am," said Sonny.

Alfred laughed. "ESPN knows, everybody knows. He called me."

"Why?" Sonny felt uneasy. Too much going on behind my back.

119

"Wanted to find out if I was going to be your manager again."

"What did you say?"

"Been there, done that," said Alfred.

Sonny wasn't sure if he liked that answer or not, but he said, "That your final answer?" just lightly enough for them to both chuckle and move on. It felt like the early sparring in a fight when you're looking for openings and weaknesses and blind spots.

"Who this kid you took in?"

"Starkey? He follows me on the bike, calls Rocky, cleans up the gym." It was the first he had thought of Starkey since he saw Alfred. He felt a twinge of guilt.

"How old is he?"

"Seventeen?" He realized he wasn't sure.

"Henry thinks the boy's not playing with a full deck."

"Starkey made things happen. Never would have broken loose from Hubbard without his e-mails, never would have gotten back in the gym without Starkey showing up." He was surprised to hear himself talk so much, with so much energy.

There was still doubt in Alfred's eyes. "He

doing what you want or pulling strings for his own reasons?"

"He talked me into calling you."

Alfred blinked at that. "Well, keep your eyes open. Sometimes rich kids get hung up on fighters, rappers, even thugs. He's a jock sniffer."

Sonny wanted to say, I feel good when he's around, like having a little brother who can help you. But he settled for a quick jab. "You rather I'm still with Malik and Boyd?"

It scored. Alfred's lips tightened, but he moved on. "Sure he's not using?"

Sonny thought about the way Starkey slipped in and out of moods, the way his voice got weird sometimes, muttering. But he said, "Never saw anything."

"Just don't be carrying for him." Alfred winked.

Sonny let himself laugh, a little loudly, he thought, but it was good to let it out on something deep in the past that only he and Alfred could laugh about. It was less than four years since Sgt. Alfred Brooks and his Port Authority narcotics squad had busted him for carrying drugs. Dumb seventeen-year-old right off the Reservation, a mule for a Times Square dope dealer.

"Long time ago."

"Things happen. You're the champ. I got a permanent ride." Alfred slapped his wheelchair. "And Jake's gone."

Sonny lost breath. That was a sucker punch, he thought. "I never got the message."

"You didn't want to—you weren't in touch. You running away again, Sonny." Alfred's thick forearms bulged as he wheeled the chair closer. "Ran off the Res, ran away from us, running from Hubbard."

Sonny's tongue was dry and filled his mouth. Finally, he said, "Starkey got me to come back."

Alfred's eyes narrowed. "Why?"

That stopped Sonny. He had never thought to ask that question, to even think about it. He didn't have an answer.

Tamika opened the door and stuck her head in. "Mom says dinner's on the table."

Saved by the bell.

He didn't make eye contact with Alfred during dinner, but he didn't have to. The girls had to catch him up on their lives. Tamika was on the basketball team, Lysa won the science fair, and when they found out he had met the rapper and the short movie star, they had a million questions. Lena kept telling them to let Sonny eat, but she looked happy. Alfred was quiet, but he was smiling, too. When the girls had to go to bed, they hugged him and whispered in his ears, "Sayonara, snotface." Then they fell down laughing.

He watched the sports news with Alfred until he went off to take care of his catheter. Sonny remembered from the old days how much maintenance Alfred's paraplegia needed: the bags and tubes and creams, the careful planned movements required for a bath.

Lena made up the bed in the den. She left a towel and a toothbrush on his pillow.

"We're glad you're here, Sonny." She opened a closet in the den. His clothes were still hanging there. There were boots and running shoes on the floor, underwear and socks in a pullout wire basket. "Knew you'd be back."

I'm glad I'm here, he thought. He enjoyed the comforting sounds of the house settling into nighttime, the whispers of TV from Alfred and Lena's bedroom, the girls stomping off to the bathroom, the gurgle of water through pipes, the scamper of squirrels on the roof. He imagined Starkey curled up in Johnson's office, dealing with the sounds outside those dirty windows. Give Starkey a call? To say what? Starkey can take care of himself. I didn't force him to come to New York. He's got Alfred's number—he can call if he needs me.

It took him a long time to fall asleep, and then he had a dream.

He was fighting a smoker in a hillbilly town, but the ring was set up outdoors, Vegas style, in the middle of Jake's auto junkyard on the Moscondaga Reservation. Half the faces in the crowd were cracker and half were Redskin, and all their mouths were open and dripping saliva, and they were all booing him as he came into the ring. They cheered as his opponent climbed up the ring steps, but Sonny couldn't see his face—it was covered with the hood of his robe. Jake and Alfred and Johnson and Hubbard and Malik and Boyd were all in his opponent's corner.

Sonny was alone. He gave the crowd the finger, but no one could see it because his boxing gloves were on. He pulled off his robe and whipped his ponytail against his bare shoulders. The crowd was laughing. He looked down. He was wearing only his jockstrap and his protective cup. He had forgotten to put on his trunks.

Doesn't matter, nothing matters.

He came out for the ring instructions. Somehow he wasn't surprised that his opponent was Starkey.

Sixteen

STARKEY WOKE UP JUMPY. He felt a cold prickle among the hairs on the back of his neck. Jake said that was a signal that enemies were about to strike. It was in The Book. Running Braves could sense events before they happened. Like Warrior Angels.

Sonny had left Alfred's phone number in case of emergency. Starkey thought about calling, but what would he say? I'm nervous? Yeah, right. Some emergency.

A night's sleep had helped, and a quarter dose of meds.

He had found a few more pills deep in the backpack.

He decided to wear the Tomahawk Kid cap. He'd been careful not to waste its powers, but he just might need it today. He slipped on the backpack and rode the bike to keep the routine going. He pedaled even harder than he did when he was following Sonny. That cleared his head, made him feel better.

Energized, he scraped some of the crusty old grime off two front windows. Johnson showed up, noticed the windows right away, and gave Starkey a little nod. Starkey wished Johnson would say something nice, but a little nod was a good start.

While Johnson drank coffee with the early birds, mostly middle-aged businessmen who hit the bag and skipped rope before work, Starkey got down on his hands and knees to scrub at some old bloodstains on the splintery wooden floor. He hoped Johnson was looking.

It was a long, slow morning without Sonny, mopping and fetching water and doing the laundry. Starkey wondered when Sonny was coming back.

If, said the Voices.

Two strangers showed up at the gym that afternoon, black guys in black leather with a lot of heavy gold around their necks and wrists. One of them had the same snake tattoo coming up his neck that Cobra Rasheed had on his chest. Johnson was out, or he'd have been at the door in a flash to check them out, Starkey thought. But none of Johnson's assistants made a move, and once Cobra hugged the two men, it was too late.

Starkey watched them swagger around the gym, making comments to each other and laughing. Sonny had told him there were rumors that Cobra was still a member of an L.A. gang he'd joined in prison. He wondered if these were fellow gang members.

Starkey forced them out of his mind and went deep into his mopping rhythm. He was starting to get it, dragging instead of pushing the ropy tangle. He needed to concentrate. He had sent Sonny back to Alfred—it was part of helping him break loose from Hubbard. It was part of his Mission. But Alfred was an old cop— those guys are paranoid. He wouldn't like Sonny having a friend. He might poison Sonny against me.

Just mop, Starkey, those are the Voices whispering to you, trying to mess you up.

"Hey, chicken chest, where's my water?"

It took him a moment to realize Cobra was yelling at him. No problem. Starkey could take Cobra yelling at him. It was almost an honor, because it was Cobra's way of getting at

Sonny. It made Starkey feel closer to Sonny to take the abuse. Cobra bullied the champ's pal because Cobra was afraid to go up against the champ.

"Afraid? What planet you on, Looney Tunes?"

Cobra's friends laughed.

A rough, unfamiliar voice said, "Save it for the fight, Rasheed. You'll need it."

"Wha' you say?" Cobra looked surprised.

The rough voice said, "Chill."

It took Starkey a moment to realize that the voice was coming out of his own mouth. He must be channeling an Archie. He felt light-headed with the honor of it.

"I'm talkin' to you," said Cobra.

That didn't register until one of the gang-bangers said, "He's talkin' to you," and flicked the bill of Starkey's Tomahawk Kid cap.

The snakes on Cobra's chest moved. Starkey hoped it was just Cobra flexing his pecs. He didn't want to go down in flames now, just when he was getting a grip.

"What do you want?" It was Starkey's normal voice now, sounding small and weak.

"You brain dead?" asked the gangbanger

who had touched the cap. "The Snake needs water. Move your little gay butt."

The other fighters and trainers in the gym were suddenly very busy. No one wanted a piece of this. Starkey felt alone. He wished Sonny were here. How do you handle a psycho thug? Even as he thought it, he knew he was saying it out loud.

"What you call me?"

Starkey's rough voice said, "You deaf as well as stupid, psycho thug?"

Cobra touched his friend's arm. "Slip it, Trey, his elevator don't go to the top."

Trey jerked his arm away. "You hear what he call me?" The snake on his neck opened its mouth and lunged at Starkey, fangs dripping with black venom. It knocked his cap off.

Starkey watched the red cap skitter across the floor before he raised the mop. He was amazed at the clarity of his mind, the Warrior Angel clicking into battle mode. He slapped the soapy, wet ropes of the mop into Trey's face, stepped back, turned the handle, and drove the stick deep into Trey's gut. The gangbanger fell backward.

Starkey broke the handle over his knee. He

held the jagged end out like a sword and screamed, "Dare you challenge a Warrior Angel?"

Cobra was whispering to his friends, "Easy, homes, no trouble here."

"There will always be trouble until the Legion of Evil surrenders to the Forces of Good." He loved hearing his thundering words echo in the hushed gym.

"See, boy's crazy," whispered Cobra, trying to herd his friends toward the door. "You don't want no piece a this."

Starkey felt the broomstick wavering in his hand. It was getting heavy. The snakes were shrinking back, mouths closing.

"What's goin' on?" Johnson stormed across the gym, dragging his leg and pulling his beard. "Put that down!"

Starkey dropped the stick as if it had been slapped out of his hand.

"Who these guys?"

"They just leavin'," said Cobra, pushing his friends toward the door.

Cursing, rolling their eyes, they swaggered out of the gym.

Starkey felt small, empty. The Archies had

abandoned him, Sonny had abandoned him, the Voices had taken over. He bent over to pick up his cap and the room tilted, the floor came up into his face.

Seventeen

SONNY WOKE BEFORE dawn, feeling a cold prickle among the hairs on the back of his neck. It was a signal that enemies were about to strike, according to Jake. More Running Braves crap. But he felt a distant anxiety, like a telephone ringing in another room. He went to the bathroom and leaned into the bathtub and ran cold water on the back of his neck. In the kitchen he made coffee and watched the Weather Channel. Might rain later. He pushed away an urge to call the gym, make sure Starkey was all right. He'd be sleeping. Think I'm the crazy one.

He went out for a long run. The suburban streets were empty, hushed, house after house with their windows shaded, their eyes closed. He was glad when dogs barked at him from inside the houses. Everybody wasn't dead.

At breakfast Alfred said, "You running too much."

"Need to get in shape."

"For a boxing match, not a marathon."

Lena said, "What Alfred's trying to say—"

"Trying to say?" Alfred sounded cranky. "I said it. He's running too much."

"That's not good enough," snapped Lena. They glared at each other, and Sonny thought, Here's two people love each other to death, not afraid to talk tough because they're tight enough to deal with anything. Be nice to have someone like that someday.

"Okay, what am I trying to say?"

"Sonny's running is less about getting physically fit than it is about trying to feel better emotionally, a kind of self-medication. This is dangerous if it means you don't deal with the issues that trouble you."

"My, my, so that's what I'm trying to say." Alfred rolled his eyes. "Amazing how these guidance counselors can read your mind."

Lena smiled and touched Sonny's hand. "It's been a hard time for you. Give yourself a break."

"Got a fight in three weeks," said Sonny.

"You might want to talk to somebody," said Lena.

The girls staggered in, sleep in their eyes,

hugged Sonny, grabbed bowls of cereal, and staggered off to the big TV in the living room.

"Saturday-morning rules," said Lena. "Only time they can watch TV on their own."

"She runs this house like Mr. Donatelli ran the gym," said Alfred.

"Have you ever thought about seeing a therapist?" Lena wasn't giving up.

"A therapist?" said Sonny, stalling.

"A sports shrink," said Alfred. "Talk about why you can't pull the trigger on combinations."

Sonny thought about Dr. Gould and remembered what Hubbard had said. *The new mot-to in sports: You gotta get shrunk to get bigger.*

"I'm serious," said Alfred.

"There was this psychologist in Vegas. Hubbard called him."

"Worked for Hubbard?" Alfred made a face.

"Doctor didn't think so. Hubbard fired him."

Lena said, "You liked him?"

"He was all right."

"Maybe he could recommend somebody in New York," said Lena. "Or I could ask around."

Sonny tried to sound joky. "I'll come talk to you."

"I'm sure I could help to a certain extent," said Lena. The way she was sitting and looking at him, Sonny thought of Dr. Gould, friendly and interested. "There's some things you just have to think about."

"Like what?" asked Sonny. He was surprised to find that he was interested, too. He thought of all the questions Starkey had asked. Or tried to ask.

"Well, the running away, to begin with. People do that for all sorts of reasons. Sometimes they're scared of being hurt, rejected, so they leave before they can be left. Sometimes they're afraid of being trapped in a relationship. They don't want to be under another person's power. Or they don't want the feeling of people depending on them."

"This is a little heavy for breakfast," said Alfred. He looked uncomfortable.

"I don't know when I'll have another chance," said Lena. "Are you okay with this, Sonny?"

He nodded. His throat was dry.

"A lot of people are afraid of something, Sonny." She reached out again and put her hand over his. "Just remember that Alfred and I are with you all the way. If you want us. Just think about it."

Lena sat back and bit her lip. Out of the corner of his eye Sonny saw Alfred give her a thumbs-up. Lena smiled. "More orange juice, Sonny?"

After a second, Sonny croaked, "Thanks."

They ate in silence for a while, glancing at the Sunday newspaper, smiling at each other, yelling at the girls to lower the TV. There was something in what Lena had said, something he would think about on his own. It could help answer his own questions about himself. But not right now. He wanted to wallow in the sweet comfort of the morning.

They were almost finished with breakfast when the front door banged open and a chubby young black man with round glasses on his owl face burst in. "Yo, Tomahawk."

"Martin Malcolm Witherspoon, the Writing Brave," said Sonny. He wondered if this was a setup. He felt too relaxed to care.

"How many eggs?" asked Lena.

"How many you got?" said Marty. He gave Sonny a light punch on the arm. "How you doin', man? Great interview on ESPN. I loved that line of yours, 'Do I look crazy to you?' Right up there with 'Go ahead, punk, make my day,' and 'You lookin' at me?'"

Sonny could tell that Marty was talking so fast because he was nervous. After a few minutes they started talking about Marty. He had transferred to a college in the city but was thinking about dropping out again to write for a new magazine that would send him overseas. Sonny was surprised that it was Alfred who urged him to stay in school, get his degree, and Lena who said take a chance if the assignment was good enough.

Sonny tuned out, let his mind go blank and open. He thought of Starkey and the calm feeling began to drain away. He began to feel restless, jittery. Maybe he was edgy from overtraining. He had run at least ten miles this morning. But Starkey's face and then his voice were pushing into his mind. Calling him back.

"I got to go," he said.

"We thought you'd stay the weekend." Lena sounded disappointed.

"People waiting on me. I'll be back."

"Wait'll I finish," said Marty. "I'll drive you."

"I can take the—"

"Let Marty drive you," said Alfred. Sonny could tell that Alfred wanted Marty and him together again. That might be okay. Like Lena said, just think about it.

Marty had his father's car, an old brown Volvo that moved through traffic like a little tank. Every other car beat it at light changes, even the SUVs.

"Jake's pickup," said Marty, "could blow this clunker off the road."

"Truck was modified," said Sonny. "Jake raced it a few times when he was younger."

"He never told me that."

"You were too busy with the Redskin hoodoo." From the corner of his eye he saw the round brown owl face wince. "Running Braves. Stonebird Mountain."

Marty laughed. "Yeah, Stonebird. I was going to go with you on the solo."

Sonny laughed. It wasn't that funny, but it helped break the ice between them. "So, you gonna stay in school?"

"Thought I might start hanging with you again."

"Write another book?"

"Bring it up-to-date for the paperback."

"That's why you showed up?" He could hear the annoyance in his voice.

"Alfred invited me," said Marty. "But I wouldn't have come if it wasn't all right with you."

"How'd you know it was all right with me?"

"Got the e-mail from your . . . assistant trainer."

"What are you talking about?" Even as he said it, Sonny figured it out. The Warrior Angel pulling strings. Helping him again.

"You didn't know?"

"Forgot," said Sonny. He didn't think it sounded convincing.

"Kid sounds like a certified nutjob."

Again he felt he needed to defend Starkey. "He helped me out, got me in gear."

"'The Warrior Angel is on his way.' Sounds like stalking by e-mail."

"Who told you that?"

"Malik."

"You talking to him?"

"For the update, yeah. You know, it's really quite common, fan becomes fixated on a celebrity."

Sonny wondered if Marty was afraid

Starkey would get in his way. "You'll get a chapter out of him."

"You think I'm just here for that?" When Sonny didn't answer, Marty kicked the Volvo into speed.

When they got to the gym, Starkey was rolled up into a ball in a corner of the couch, his knees against his chest, hugging his elbows. His face was hidden by the bill of a ratty old red cap.

"He been like this, won't talk," said Johnson. "Kid's a lunatic. Don't want him around no more."

"Let me alone with him," said Sonny. He waited until Johnson left. "You okay?"

Starkey looked up. "Who's that?"

Sonny realized that Marty had come into the room behind him. "Marty Witherspoon."

"The man who wrote The Book?"

Marty puffed up and patted Starkey's shoulder. "We're here now—everything's gonna be fine."

"Starkey, what happened?"

"Cobra's friends. I . . . kind of lost it. Where were you?"

Everyone wanted a piece of him. Just like

always. "Just stay here, be cool. I'll talk to Johnson." When he saw Starkey squinting at Marty, he said, "Talk to the great writer. The two of you deserve each other."

He couldn't keep the anger out of his voice.

Eighteen

THE VOICES WERE SOFT but insistent, murmuring from the faces on old fight posters, whispering from the peeled patches on the ceiling, warning Starkey to be watchful, to be ready to run. He couldn't trust anyone anymore.

Marty Witherspoon had asked too many questions yesterday. It was more like an interview than a conversation. Why? What had Sonny talked about with Alfred? He had talked with Johnson for a long time before he'd come back to the office and said that Starkey could stay, but one more outburst and he'd have to leave.

They want to get rid of you, Starkeeeeee.

Mopping helped. He poured extra disinfectant into the water so the fumes were needles in his nose. He scrubbed the grimy wooden floor until his back and shoulders ached, until his thighs quivered, welcoming the pain that wiped out all other thoughts. He focused on rubbing out the old brown bloodstains until the floor-boards rose and went snaky and the Voices slipped up from the cracks.

Starkeeeeee, they want to send you back to the Family Place, baaack to Whitmore, baaaaaack to Stepdad's slammer.

He tried a trick that sometimes worked, squeezing the Voices out of his brain, like wringing the mop, squeezing them to the inside of his skull, then pushing them out his ears by silently chanting, I am on a Mission for the Creator, I am a Warrior Angel on a Mission for the Creator.

"That some kind of song?" asked Johnson. Starkey hadn't seen him come up.

"Helps me mop." What else could he say?

"Just so it ain't rap."

If he could concentrate on something else, he could keep the Voices at bay. Out on the bike following Sonny at dawn today was good, but the long morning until the professional trainers and fighters filled the gym was hard. It got better when they stomped in, shouting, crowd-ing the room with their busy noise, heavy bags thumping, the *slap-slap-slap* of jump ropes, the *rat-a-ta-ta-tat* of the peanut bags, bells, buzzers, the amped music all filling his mind with rhythms that pushed the Voices and the shape-shifters into the nooks and crannies of his skull.

The boxers were mostly black and Latino, and some of them looked him over with narrow eyes, as if they wondered why a white kid was scrubbing the floor. When they tossed him a towel or a water bottle to fill, they just grunted. But every so often Sonny would pass by and say something to him, which made him cool to everyone and he felt good.

You think he really cares about you? the Voices asked.

He knows I'm here to help him.

Help him clean the gym? He left you alone as soon as he could.

He passed Cobra shadowboxing. The reflection in the mirror glared at him, and the two snakes on his chest opened their mouths wider. Their fangs dripped. He hurried toward the washer and dryer with a mountain of towels.

Hubbard's voice filled the gym before Starkey saw him. "No fear, I'm here, at the camp of the champ. I come in peace."

Cobra growled, "You could leave in pieces."

"Always liked that mean streak of yours, Rasheed. Tells me I can count on you in the late rounds when the going gets tough."

The snakes relaxed on Cobra's chest, smiled. Starkey thought, Hubbard's the snake, world's fattest snake. He recognized the two young men, one white, one black, trailing behind him. The idiot managers, Boyd and Malik.

Hubbard in person was bigger, shinier than he appeared on TV. Trainers and boxers flocked around him. Nobody was going to dis the most important promoter in the sport. Even Johnson grudgingly shook hands with Hubbard.

"You doin' a fine job, Henry," boomed Hubbard. "You are keeping up the standards of Mr. Donatelli."

"Some of the old dirt still here too," said Malik, toeing the inlaid grit on the wooden floor.

Starkey snapped, "That old dirt knows more about boxing than you do."

Malik looked up, eyes furiously red, his teeth growing. Starkey's hands tightened on the mop handle as Malik's body swelled and he started toward him.

"That mop boy is right," said Hubbard. "There's history in this dirt, ambience we call it. Where's Sonny?"

He sauntered across the gym floor to where Sonny was pounding the heavy bag and carefully ignoring him. "You okay, Sonny? Anything we can do for you?"

Don't look at him, thought Starkey.

"Bygones are gone by, champ. I just want you to know I got no hard feelings."

Don't answer him, thought Starkey.

"I got hard feelings."

"I'm counting on that, and you will express them when you tear down The Wall." Hubbard flapped his arms to create a space around himself and Sonny. Everyone backed away. He lowered his voice so Starkey couldn't hear.

But he could imagine what Hubbard was saying: You got to get rid of that mop boy. Warrior Angels are trouble. They are crazy. They will drag you down.

Starkey went into the laundry room and held on to the dryer until the heat and the throbbing metal drove everything else out of his head.

Nineteen

JOHNSON SAID, "He makes everybody nervous."
They stood in Johnson's office watching as
Starkey moved around the gym, crouched,
throwing quick looks over either shoulder as he
scooped up used towels, refilled water bottles,
mopped up pools of sweat. He looked different
to Sonny, more like a scuttling crab than the
confident loudmouth who had swaggered into
the gym less than a week ago.

"Does his work," said Sonny.

"Alfred says he's a time bomb."

"Alfred's never seen him."

"Told him about the boy. Gives me the
heebie-jeebies."

Starkey looked as jumpy as a Reservation
dog. He was muttering to himself. But Sonny
couldn't just let him be driven out of the gym.
Where would he go?

"I can't just send him away."

"You can't baby-sit him neither," said

Johnson. "Or expect me to."

"Maybe I need to go to another gym." Even as he said it, he knew it made no sense. Starkey had gotten him back here, where he belonged.

Johnson sighed and pulled his beard. "Sonny, you know I'm right."

He knew Johnson was right. Title fight around the corner, he'd be out of the gym more and more for appearances and meetings and interviews. While Starkey was getting weirder and weirder.

Starkey was quiet that night at dinner. Hunched over the table, his body was a clenched fist, head down, elbows against his chest. His hands dangled from his wrists as he picked at chicken from Kim's. After a while he looked up and said, "You eating?"

"Eating at Johnson's," said Sonny, "while we look at tapes."

"Why not here?"

"Alfred can't get up these stairs anymore."

"They don't like me." Starkey's voice sounded flat, a computerized voice.

"Don't worry about it."

"They want you to get rid of me."

149

"Just be cool."

"Cooool?" Starkey's voice changed, rose.

"Will you bag that crazy voice?"

"You don't lissss-ten to meeee."

"Not when you talk like that."

"You're not ready for The Waaaaaallllllll."

"Thanks for the pep talk."

"Tooooo soooon."

Sonny left him yelling at the ceiling. I owe this guy, he thought. But I can't deal with this right now.

Johnson had an apartment a few blocks from the gym, four bedrooms and three bathrooms and a living room big enough for a baby grand piano. One of his kids was a composer. Alfred and Marty were already there, parked in front of the monster TV, rewinding back and forth through the eighth round of the fight with The Wall.

Alfred barely looked up as Sonny walked in. "Here's where you won the title, Sonny. Floyd lost heart right here. He was running out of steam and you were getting stronger."

"The jab—you never stopped pumping it in his face," said Johnson, coming in with plates of cold poached salmon and salad. "Eleanor cooked this. She had to go to a community board meeting. Said to say hello."

Sonny tried to concentrate, but he kept thinking about Starkey, hunched over the table, alone in the gym. What was he going to do? And was Starkey right? Was he fighting too soon?

"He's going to be expecting the jab," said Alfred, "and he's going to be looking for the hook to follow. That was the pattern here, and he'll be looking at the same tapes."

Marty stuffed fish into his mouth. "Mmm, real moist. Fool him: Stay with the jab and hook combination, since they'll be expecting us to change the plan."

"Don't complicate this," said Johnson.

"Boxing is chess with blood," said Marty.

"You better stick to chess," said Alfred, poking Marty, "before I shed some of your blood."

An old joke. They all laughed. Sonny felt warmed by being back with them, but trapped, too. Can you feel two emotions at the same time? Maybe I'm the crazy one. A part of me wants to stay here, part of me wants to get out.

Sonny nodded, but he wasn't really listening as they argued strategy through dinner. His ears didn't perk up until Alfred said, "So what are you doing about the stalker?"

"He's not a stalker. . . ."

"He tracked you down," said Alfred. "Don't matter if he did it by shoe leather or e-mail."

"It's my problem," said Sonny.

Johnson said, "All our problem, Sonny. We got a fight coming up."

"I'm not going to just dump him."

Alfred said, "You done that before."

He was grateful when Marty said, "Sonny wouldn't be here without the kid."

"Find out where he came from," said Alfred. "I'll call them to send out the butterfly nets."

"He helped me," said Sonny.

"So help him," said Johnson. "Get him back where they can take care of him proper."

Alfred said, "You know where he was running from?"

Sonny lied. "No."

On his way up the stairs he heard Starkey grunting in the darkness. When he turned on the gym lights, he saw Starkey on his hands and

knees, scrubbing old bloodstains. He was wearing the ratty old red cap backward.

"What are you doing?"

"Gotta finish before they come."

"Who?" He knew he didn't want to know.

"The Legion."

"Better not talk like that in front of Johnson
and the others."

"It doesn't matter, Sonny. The Legion got to
them. They're not on your side. They're using
you."

"Get some sleep."

"They want you to lose. Hubbard wants you
to lose, set up the third fight, the big one."

Sonny felt a cold spot in his stomach. Can't
hear this now. "They wouldn't do that."

"They know you're not ready for this fight.
You're not in shape, your head's not there yet."

"You're talking crazy."

Starkey stood up, swaying. "Listen to
meeeeeeeee." He kicked over the metal bucket.
Ammonia fumes rose off the water sloshing
over the wooden floor.

Sonny grabbed his arms, but Starkey
wrenched free. He began running around the
gym, kicking over buckets, hurling water

bottles against the walls, beating the bags. "Listen beeeforrrre they get meeeeeee."

It took longer than Sonny expected for Starkey's energy to run down. He waited until Starkey stopped and hugged a heavy bag, then wrapped his arms around Starkey's waist. Starkey moaned, "Noooooooooooooo," but he didn't struggle as Sonny pried him loose and carried him into Johnson's office. He dumped Starkey on the couch and held him until he fell asleep.

The cold spot grew to fill Sonny's stomach and chest. Stalker, savior, both. What am I gonna do? I owe him. But I can't baby-sit him.

Maybe Alfred and Johnson are right. Get him to the people who can help him.

Twenty

THE VOICES WOKE HIM, murmuring so softly, he could not understand what they were saying.

The meds were all gone but that didn't matter. He would never be free of the Voices.

As long as he lived, they would be in his head.

It was the longest day he could remember. He was hanging on by his fingernails. Riding the bike behind Sonny, he felt the streets flow under the quivering tires, oceans of streets in unending waves. He hid in the laundry room as reporters and camera crews clustered around Sonny, watched him spar with Dave the Fave, interviewed everybody in the gym, even Cobra. The red cap helped, but its powers were failing.

The snakes were sticking their tongues out at him.

Through the afternoon Starkey watched the

clock, but the hands mocked him, quivering, spinning backwards. I can't hold on much longer.

I can't let the Legion take me over.

At five o'clock Sonny said, "You'll be okay?"

He'd never asked that before. What's he mean? We can smell trouble, Warrior Angels and Running Braves. Is he trying to warn me? What is he trying to tell me?

"I'm not trying to tell you anything. Be back real late. The boxing writers' dinner at the Hilton."

Then he was gone.

Then everybody was gone.

Starkey held the cap down on his head, pressing his thumbs into his temples. That helped sometimes, quieting the throbbing inside his skull. Not this time.

He checked the backpack—laptop, The Book—before he slipped it on. Better be ready for anything.

It was dark in the gym. He heard the old bloodstains bubble up from the wooden floor. He was looking for the mop when the hairs stood up on the back of his neck.

The door burst open and the lights exploded

on.

"Stay calm, Richard. Everything's going to be all right."

Three big men dressed almost identically in double-breasted black blazers and black T-shirts were marching across the gym. They wore radio headsets. They looked like the security goons that Stepdad's company hired for parties and concerts.

A middle-aged couple was right behind them, jumping around to peer over and around their broad backs. Somebody's parents, Starkey thought.

Somebody's mother shouted, "Richard . . ."

Starkey heard himself wail, "Nooooooo . . ."

The head goon shouted, "Collect 'im." Fire came out of his eyes.

"Don't hurt my son," screamed Somebody's Mom.

"For God's sake, Cynthia, let them do their job," yelled Somebody's Stepdad.

Starkey found the mop and swung it, but the goons surrounded him. They were dancing and laughing, black lava pouring out of their open mouths, chanting, "Gotchagotchagotcha, angel."

157

You're no Warrior Angel, said the Voices. You're a simpleton, a fool, a crazy boy.

That's why Sonny bailed on you and ratted you out.

Twenty-one

SONNY WAS HUNGRY, clearheaded, on edge. He was up on the balls of his feet, jiggling, making it hard for Johnson to tape his hands. But Johnson was grinning and so was Alfred. Like old times almost. Malik and Boyd were sulking in a corner of the dressing room with nothing to do. Red Eagle had been banished to the corridor. Next fight they'll all be gone, out of my contract, out of my life.

"Jab," said Johnson, holding up a hand. He nodded as Sonny's taped fist smacked into his palm. "That's it. Again. Just like that. You'll take down The Wall one brick at a time."

"Hold that thought, young gentleman," said Alfred. "Only one thing in your mind. How we gonna make The Wall come tumbling down? Again."

Now they never stopped talking, low and urgent, as the commissioner signed the tape, as the gloves went on, as the door banged open and someone yelled, "Five minutes," and then they were out in the arena, the television lights cooking the air.

He thought of the last time he had walked out into this Vegas parking lot, a zombie in a murky brown cloud. This time his nerves tingled, the thoughts bounced against the inside of his skull. He wondered if Starkey was listening to the fight. Been three weeks since I saw him last.

He probably thinks I called the people who snatched him. Kim saw them driving away in two limos that night. Dr. Gould said it would have been all right if I had called them. He's okay, that shrink. He didn't want to get involved, but he found out that Starkey was in the hospital. Some girl from the Family Place spotted him on TV and helped his parents arrange the snatch. Felt relieved that somebody else was taking care of Starkey. Back from the writers' dinner that night, when he wasn't there, I was almost glad. And then I had to focus on the fight.

Alfred's voice broke through. "Stick and move."

"To the left, always to your left," said

Johnson, and then Sonny was in the ring, nodding back at The Wall, they were both too professional to glare like gangstas, that man is HUGE. Sonny heard a voice, sounded just like Starkey, "Bigger the wall, the harder they fall," made him laugh, and Johnson grunted, "Don't get cocky on me, boy," and Sonny let the parade of celebrities slap his gloves, the rap singer and the action hero, "Sayonara, snotface," they said in unison, they are friends now, but Sonny kept thinking, Jab and go left, not letting the tattoos and the breasts and the gold teeth steal his concentration. Cobra got a round of applause from the crowd as he swaggered into the ring. He'd won his fight with a second-round knockout. As he tapped Sonny's gloves, he whispered, "Win, baby. I got next."

Bells rang, the ring was cleared. The announcer pulled down the microphone. "And now, the main event, for the heavyweight championship of the world . . . in the blue trunks, the former heavyweight champion, at two hundred twenty-eight pounds, Floyd . . . The Wallllll . . . Hallllll."

The crowd was up and stomping, cheering, whistling.

161

"In the red trunks, youngest heavyweight champion in history, at two hundred ten pounds, the Tomahawk Kid, Son-neeeeeeeeeeee Bear."

In the avalanche of sound sweeping over the ring, he heard Johnson's needle-sharp, "First round, feel him out," and Alfred, shouting up from his wheelchair at the ring steps, "Stick and move, stick and move," and then they were standing in the middle of the ring and the referee was giving the usual instructions about neutral corners and break when told, and The Wall nodded, the mother blocked out the light, he is HUGE, let's get it on already, and then, finally, the bell.

Through earpiece of the tiny radio, Starkey heard, "The Wall acts like Sonny's jabs are just green flies at the picnic."

He closed his eyes and imagined that Sonny looked sharp, nothing like the zombie who had fought Navy Crockett. But The Wall is too strong to push around in the early rounds. No quick knockout here. Yet even if Sonny has the patience, does he have the endurance to go the distance? Is he ready?

"Richard?" said Dr. Raphael.

Reluctantly, he pulled out the earpiece. It had taken a week of begging and good behavior to get the little radio. Don't blow it now.

Dr. Raphael said, "I thought we had trust." He was holding up the little plastic specimen cup. The daily urine test. "I'm very disappointed, Richard."

They always say something like that. To make you feel guilty. Like bagging meds is a crime against them.

"I wouldn't have been able to concentrate on the fight."

"The medicine shuts down the voices."

"But I need to hear the Voices so I can counteract them."

"That's courageous, Richard, but it might not be in your best interests right now." He had a needle.

"This is really important to me, Dr. Raphael. You've seen how I behaved so I could hear the fight. As soon as the fight's over, I'll take whatever you want." The doctor was flicking the air out of the syringe. I don't want to have to slug him. Talk fast, Starkey. Angels have magic tongues. "I want to get better, Dr. Raphael. You

163

think I want to be trapped in this Warrior Angel
fantasy the rest of my life?"

That stopped him. "You were making
progress."

"I still am. But I know I need to hear this
fight if I'm to make more progress. I need to
bond with the reality." That was good. Made
him blink. "And tomorrow, you can start any
protocol you want, with my total cooperation."

Dr. Raphael lowered the needle. "Your parents agree with me that electroconvulsive therapy could be useful."

Starkey winked. "I'm shocked." Cool?

It took the doctor a minute to chuckle. Too
dumb to be Legion. "I have faith in you,
Richard."

He squeezed Starkey's shoulder on the way
out.

Starkey got the earpiece back in. He hadn't
missed much.

Sonny jabbed and moved away from The
Wall's powerhouse left hook, keeping his own
left up to block The Wall's straight right. He
danced on the balls of his feet as The Wall kept
turning, flat-footed. By the third round the

crowd in the arena was booing. No hard punches had been landed. They wanted some action, some blood. They always do. Someone in the front row sang a waltz tune, and the section picked it up.

Keep jabbing and moving, sure, but how long before The Wall just bulls forward, clinches, tries to drive me into the ropes? Have to confuse him, get The Wall angry, frustrated, have him lunge and commit himself to bad punches, humiliate him, bang him around, run him into a corner.

Sonny sidestepped right, paused just long enough to bait The Wall into throwing a quick, clumsy hook. He let it slip past his ear, then stepped forward and drove a right into The Wall's stomach. As the big man leaned forward, Sonny stepped back and chopped two lefts to his temple, then a hard right to his chin. The Wall staggered back and the crowd roared. He shook it off. It meant nothing, but it was a start.

Starkey imagined the hugeness of The Wall pressing in on Sonny, cutting off the ring, trying to surround him. He seemed even bigger than the last time. This time he hadn't taken Sonny lightly, dismissed him as an overhyped kid he could easily crush. The Wall had trained hard, rebuilt himself into the immovable object who had never lost a fight, who had never even been knocked down, until Sonny took away his title.

It feels, thought Starkey, as if Sonny is . . . as if we are . . . as if I am pounding on bricks.

The new night nurse's bearded face appeared in the doorway, mounted on an enormous body draped in white. He looked like a bobblehead snowbank. Like to melt his nasty ass. Even after Dr. Raphael okayed the little radio—a Stepdad special that picked up the Armed Forces radio signal that got free title fights—the nurse had his grubby hand out. It had taken more than a few Locs 'n' Bagels CDs to buy him off. He wouldn't give Starkey the backpack with the red cap and The Book and the laptop, even though Dr. Raphael said Starkey could have it back. The nurse was holding out for a few bucks. At least the man was too lazy to feel around the binding of The Book. Dishonest and dumb. Lucky me. I can work with that.

Starkey smiled and waved at him. He scowled and lumbered away.

*   *   *

It seemed to Sonny as if every jab was answered with a stiff right hand from Floyd. In the beginning he skipped easily out of the way, jabbing and dancing back or to the side, letting Floyd lurch awkwardly after his missed punch. Then, almost imperceptibly, as the pace of the fight slowed, Sonny would slip the punch by tilting his head to the right and let Floyd's glove fly harmlessly over his left shoulder. By the eighth round, the rights began to make contact, glance off his shoulder, first skim away, then bounce, then bruise bone.

He welcomed the pain, breathed into it, tried to use it to stay zoned, up on the balls of his feet, to keep his combinations rattling. But he was tired. He was losing concentration. He felt The Wall grow and surround him. Trapped inside The Wall. How do I get out? And where do I go?

"Stick and move."

Starkey felt Sonny's shoulder grow numb. A razor edge of pain sliced down his arm to his fingertips. Sonny was pushing the jab more than firing it. He was tired. He wasn't ready for this fight.

The radio announcer's voice was hot and urgent. He sounded excited at the possibility that The Wall might win back his title. He kept saying that Floyd had been a popular champion, a soft-spoken African-American Christian, a home-loving family man who visited hospitals and Army bases and did public service commercials on the importance of learning how to read. Just the kind of person who should be heavyweight champion of the world.

"A real role model," he said. "As a man, The Wall is solid. And he's looking solid in the ring tonight."

Too much up against us, thought Starkey. If the radio announcer feels this way, the referee and the judges probably do too. That means Sonny is going to have to knock out The Wall to win, he's not going to get the benefit of points.

Go for it, Sonny, take him, knock down The Wall.

Sonny thought, I'm going to have to go for it. Try to knock him out. The bricks are not coming loose. And I am getting tired.

Alfred was yelling, "Reach down, Sonny, don't be fading now," and Johnson, nose to nose, said, "Suck it up," and slapped his face. The cut man waved a bottle under his nose that sent a chemical hot wire up into his brain. When the bell rang for the next round, he dropped an ice cube down Sonny's trunks.

His legs felt like cement poles. The Wall shook him with a quick left-right, but he managed to duck away from the hook. That could have ended it, Sonny. Wake up!

Starkey felt cold and hot. It was now or never, forget about dismantling The Wall brick by brick, there was no time for that anymore, it was knock him out in this round or lose the title, youngest former champion in history, and then who are we?

If Sonny loses, I lose.

The Voices win.

And then there will be only one way left to save Sonny and complete the Mission.

Sonny could see The Wall was tired too. His tree-trunk legs were taking root, the enormous chest was heaving for air, his right eye was

169

closed from a hundred jabs that had gotten through his guard. His face was lumpy and bloody. He grunted from the pain and effort of raising his cannon arms.

Sonny felt a surge of energy. The power ran down his shoulders into his arms, down his spine into his legs. He danced into range, easily blocked Floyd's slow, looping hook with his right arm, and slammed a hook of his own deep into Floyd's side. The Wall wavered.

"Right, one," screamed Alfred.

Sonny set his feet and fired the short right to Floyd's jaw, put his legs and hips and butt into it, watched it slam into the top of The Wall and drive him back against the ropes.

"Do it," screamed Johnson and Alfred and Starkey.

The roar of the crowd pushed him forward like a surfer's wave, finish him off. Sonny tried to pound Floyd off the ropes, to hammer him into the ground, but his arms were so sore and the gloves on his hands were so heavy and punching through the water was so slow. He didn't have enough left to knock down The Wall.

The Wall stood up and they were toe to toe

and forehead to forehead and banging each other in slow motion, pawing each other until the bell rang and they fell into each other's arms murmuring, "Good fight."

Their cornermen swarmed into the ring to wait for the officials' decision.

Listening to the radio announcers read their scorecards, Starkey felt sad but not surprised. They liked The Wall because he was a better interview subject, friendlier. Sonny was a quiet guy, a loner. He didn't even have a posse! Hard to figure.

They don't understand him, thought Starkey. Who knew him better than I did? And now . . .

The crowd cheered the decision, unanimous for The Wall.

At ringside, a radio reporter asked, "How do you feel, Sonny Bear, youngest ex-champion in heavyweight history?"

What sounded like Alfred's voice shouted, "Dumb question," but Hubbard quickly took over and said, "Gooood question! Sonny will answer that when he tries to become the youngest man ever to regain the throne."

171

"There's a rematch?"

"The Wall has a contract with me," said Hubbard.

Starkey felt a prick of admiration for the promoter. *Hubbard is the pick of the Legion. The Archies chose me to best him, and I can't let them down.*

Sonny was too tired to think. "What you think?"

Alfred said, "We'll deal with Hubbard in the morning."

"That's what I think," said Johnson.

Sonny said, "Where's Malik? I need his laptop."

He knew there would be a message telling him what to do next.

The night nurse came in with a paper cup of pills.

Starkey said, "I need to send an e-mail." The message was already moving around inside his head like a buzzing fly: *Pick up the stones.*

"In the morning," said the nurse. "We'll ask Dr. Raphael—"

"Four words. You can watch me send them

from the computer in the nurse's station."

When the nurse shook his head, Starkey said, "Be just one minute and then I'll take my pills."

The nurse rattled the cup. "Let's go—busy night."

"I send four words and then I take the pills. Otherwise you spend half the night setting up the IV." He tried to sound firm without making it sound like a direct challenge.

The nurse glared at him. Starkey bit his lip so he wouldn't laugh. You call that intimidation, whale belly? This Angel stood up to Cobra's homies.

Starkey dropped his eyes, peeked from a corner. More than two dozen keys hung from one big ring looped carelessly over the nurse's walkie-talkie antenna. Looked like house keys, car keys, patient room keys, drug box keys. Man should be fired. But not until I borrow a few of those keys.

"So?" Another cup to rattle.

"Four little words and we both have a good night."

When the nurse sighed, Starkey knew he had it. Night staff are either very good or very

bad, and this one is in a league of his own.
Won't last long.

Long enough for me to get my stuff and
elope.

But first, *Pick up the stones,* four little words
to save Sonny and complete the Mission.

Twenty-two

ONNY FOUND MOST of the stones in the dry creek beds deep in the Reservation. Centuries of rushing water had rubbed them round and smooth. A Running Brave must be able to close both hands over each of the stones he carries on his solo climb up Stonebird. One hundred pounds of stones in a heavy-duty backpack.

He filled three canteens with water and began the climb.

The early going was easy, the trail wide and gently sloped. After three days he was still sore from the fight. His hips and shoulders complained each time he twisted to take a stone from the pack, then bent to place it alongside the trail.

Each stone left behind represented another useless burden cast off on the climb to manhood.

Arrogance. Meanness. Selfishness.

A Running Brave, on a mission for the Nation, cannot be slowed by angers and foolishness and childish fears.

As he moved up the mountain, the weight of the backpack lightened. By the time the trail became narrow and steep, the backpack was half empty, stones strung out behind him like pearls on a string. He kept his mind empty as he climbed, concentrating on the path, on the stones, on keeping his mouth closed and breathing through his nose. He drank often but sparingly.

He reached the peak just before twilight, exhausted from the climb, from the fight, from the last few weeks. He found a tall rock still warm from the sun and sat against it.

The Res looked different from the last time he'd been here, a year ago. Scattered among the shacks and trailers were new suburban-style homes, a few big ones with white columns on the front porches. Gambling money.

And looming over all, the Hiawatha Hotel and Casino. When he had fought The Wall here last year to win the title, the roof wasn't finished on the first building. Now there were three huge hotel buildings, surrounded by thousands of cars and buses.

The sun slipped behind a distant mountain, leaving an orange smear. He heard animals scurrying in the rocks below him. A young man chosen to be a Running Brave spends the night alone with the snakes and wolves and bears and mountain lions, and with the scariest creatures of all, the dark shapes that lurk in the corners of his mind.

On the way down, if he was ready to accept the honor, he would pick up his stones, symbolic of a willingness to assume his heavy new responsibilities as a warrior-diplomat for the Nation. A man of his people. It had been Jake's dream that he carry on that tradition.

It had always seemed like such crap.

But not to Starkey. Poor Starkey, looking for something to hold on to while his devils chased him. In his mind the Running Braves became the Warrior Angels for him. All from Marty's book. Took me so long to figure that out. Am I stupid or am I not paying attention to other people's feelings? To my own?

I've got to take control of my life. Keep the monster and the dark shadow at the end of my jab. It doesn't always have to be one or the other, the anger or the murk. And I don't always have to be running away.

Got to get in shape, win the title back.

Got to help Starkey.

Got to come through for him the way he kept coming through for me. Even after they busted him, he reached out to me.

Pick up the stones.

Start from the beginning. This time do it right.

I'll visit him when I go back.

Sonny looked at the sky, so near and black and starry it seemed unreal, an animated video sky. How long since he had seen stars? He'd seen no stars in Harlem or Vegas.

He imagined his body a tepee crowded with dancers around a cookfire. Where did that come from? Good feeling.

He wished he had someone to share that with. He thought of Alfred and Lena. He thought of Starkey.

The bus from New York went right to the front door of the Hiawatha Hotel and Casino. Starkey was first off, hurrying to the high-speed outside elevator that zoomed up to the observation tower. He spotted Jake's junkyard right away. The description in The Book made it easy. It was just below the highest mountain on the Reservation. Stonebird.

He mingled with the casino crowd until dark, then made his way around the parking lots, over fences, through fields until he reached the junkyard. The ancient Cadillac was exactly where The Book said it would be. It stank from mildew and cats. Starkey climbed into the rotted-out backseat. Young Sonny had once hidden here and drawn pictures.

Starkey thought the stink and the excitement would keep him awake all night, but he fell asleep immediately.

Ally was in the racing dream, although it didn't look like her. She was carrying the green flag.

"Pedal-to-the-metal time," she said. "You ready?"

Starkey and Sonny gave her the thumbs-up. Ally raised the flag.

They floored the clutches and feathered the accelerators, a quarter inch deeper with each light pump until the pedals were down and the engines were howling. When the muscles in

Ally's forearm tensed, Starkey began to let the clutch up. By the time the flag was down, he was in gear. The crowd was screaming.

Clean start. Sonny bucked ahead as they passed Ally, which was expected. His Ford had awesome pickup. But they were door to door by the time the headlights found the bales. They looked at each other and nodded at the same time. Go for it!

Starkey didn't know who had first called it the Edge, but racers had been daring it since the quarry opened. That's all the Edge was, the rim of the town's limestone quarry, a huge dark hole in the ground a hundred feet deep.

Racing the Edge was simple. The winner was the car that stopped closer to the Edge. The driver who chickened out, and stopped first, lost. But if you went too far, you shot over the rim and died in a fiery crash below.

They drove around the bales and headed for the rim of the quarry, black nothingness a football field ahead. They were still door to door. Sonny and Starkey looked at each other. Neither of them wanted to lose this one. Sonny yelled something Starkey couldn't hear over the engine.

Ally stepped in front of Starkey's car.

He swerved around her. Now he was headed into Sonny's car. He tried to shout a warning, but his tongue was stuck to the roof of his mouth.

The rim was coming up fast. If he braked, he'd lose the race—if he didn't, he'd ram into Sonny and drive him over the Edge.

Starkey woke up sweating. The dream had made it clear. There was only one way to complete the Mission.

He worked the razor blade out of the binding of The Book. The blade was still very sharp. Just touching it with his thumb drew blood.

At dawn Sonny began to move back down the mountain, picking up his stones. He was stiff and sore, but he felt good. He had the answer he had come for.

The answer was that there was no answer. You just have to keep finding your way. Let other people help you. Help other people.

The monster and the dark shadow will always be lurking out there. Starkey's Voices will always be waiting in ambush. All we can do is never give up, keep punching, move on, and watch for signs.

Got to tell Starkey that.

The pack grew heavier as he trudged down Stonebird. He staggered to the trail head under the hundred-pound weight, slipped it off, rested, then dragged the pack of rocks to the yard of Jake's old house. He would pile the rocks in a ceremonial mound on Jake's grave. The old man would like that.

He was not surprised to find a sign waiting for him on top of Jake's mailbox. It was a marked-up, dog-eared copy of *The Tomahawk Kid*. The book's binding was ripped open.

Another sign. Starkey's backpack rested against the junkyard's open gate. The laptop was in the pack. That's a bad sign, thought Sonny. The Warrior Angel wouldn't leave his laptop unless he doesn't need it anymore.

"Starkey?"

The sound bounced off the old hulks. Sonny began to run, weaving among the wrecked cars. He sensed danger. The hair prickled on the back of his neck and his senses were Running Brave sharp. He smelled the rotting rubber tires and heard the rust flaking off the sagging carcasses. As he ran deeper into the junkyard, he began to wonder if he was the hunter or the prey.

"Starkey?"

Sign. A dirty, sweat-stained red baseball cap was perched on the roof of a Cadillac. He remembered that old corpse.

He heard Starkey before he saw him, breathing hard in the backseat.

"I used to hide in this one."

"It was in The Book," said Starkey. He was curled up.

"Come on out."

"Why?"

"We need to talk."

Sonny peered into the car. Starkey was folded into a corner of the backseat, his bony knees jammed up against his chest. His long thin face was very pale, his long dark hair tangled and damp. He held something between the thumb and forefinger of his right hand.

"They're coming to get me."

"Moscondaga is a sovereign nation, Starkey—not even U.S. Marshals can come on this land without permission."

Starkey's laugh was an ugly snort. "You don't get it, Sonny. The Legion is out there."

Dogs barked at the wind in the trees. Sonny worked his head and shoulders into the back. "I'm here, man. Dare them to get past me."

"Too many." Starkey raised his hand. There was a razor blade between his fingers. He pressed it against the side of his throat. Near the jugular vein, thought Sonny. He had already cut himself. A single thread of blood trickled down his throat.

"We can take 'em. Running Braves and Warrior Angels."

"There are no Warrior Angels."

"Gotta be. I know there are Running Braves."

"Too late. Can't let 'em get me."

"We got backup, Starkey. We got Alfred and Marty and Johnson. Dr. Gould. Even that slick-ass Hubbard can help us. All on our side, all down with the Warrior Angel."

"Not enough. I got to do this, Sonny. The battle's over." The calm in Starkey's voice was chilling. He's decided, realized Sonny, to kill himself. Keep talking.

"Battle's not over, Starkey, just started." Sonny forced himself to breathe, to swallow down the fear. "Can't quit now."

184

Starkey drew another line of blood down his throat. "I got to do this before they take me."

Sonny was close enough to grab Starkey's razor hand, but he wasn't sure he'd be fast enough to stop him from making that one fatal cut. Starkey had begun another line of blood, a little deeper this time.

Try something else. "One thing I don't get, Starkey. You had to come all the way up here to kill yourself?"

Starkey's voice cracked. "I came up to kill you, Sonny. You don't know how bad it is when the Voices tell you what to do and you can't stop it."

"But you didn't kill me. You're fighting them right now." Sonny touched Starkey's knee. It was vibrating. "We can fight them together. We got to keep going. Hang on. It's not like a boxing match, twelve rounds or less. This shit goes on and on forever. It's life."

This time it sounded like a laugh coming through Starkey's nose.

"Sonny made a speech."

"All I got. Come on, let's get out of this hole."

"So the shrinks can put me in another one?"

185

It sounded like a real question to Sonny. And Starkey was listening for the answer.

"Whatever it takes."

"Zap my brains?"

"I'll be with you all the way."

"Why?" He lowered the razor to stare at Sonny. His eyes jiggled in their red-rimmed sockets.

"You saved me, man. My turn now."

"I let you down." He started to lift the razor back to his throat. "I didn't complete the Mission."

Sonny fired the jab, open handed, and wrapped his fingers around Starkey's. He felt the bite of the razor. But he had it.

"Warrior Angel came to save me and you did. You ever think what you saved me for?"

"What?" Starkey didn't struggle.

"You saved me so I could save you. That's how you complete the Mission." Sonny reached in with his right hand and gripped Starkey's wrist before he opened his left hand and plucked out the razor. He threw it out the window. "Let's go, little brother."

Starkey began to cry as Sonny pulled him out into the sunlight.